CHARLES BUKOWSKI

what matters most is how well you walk through the fire.

ecco

An Imprint of HarperCollinsPublishers

HarperCollins books may be purchased for educational, business, or sales promotional use. For information, please e-mail the Special Markets Department at SPsales@harpercollins.com.

First Ecco edition 2002
Previously published by Black Sparrow Press

ACKNOWLEDGMENTS

These poems, written between 1970 and 1990, are part of an archive that Charles Bukowski left to be published after his death.

On behalf of the author, the publisher would like to thank the editors of the periodicals where some of these poems first appeared.

Coverphotograph taken by Linda Lee Bukowski in Los Angeles in 1999.

LIBRARY OF CONGRESS CATALOGING-IN-PUBLICATION DATA

Bukowski, Charles. 1920-1994.
    What matters most is how well you walk through the fire / Charles Bukowski.
        p.   cm.
    ISBN 1-57423-105-7 (pbk.: alk. paper).
    ISBN 1-57423-106-5 (cloth: alk. paper)
    I. Title.
PS3552.U4 W48   1999
811'.54—dc21   99-47459
                                                                                        CIP

22 23 24 25 26 LBC 39 38 37 36 35

for Marina Louise Bukowski

table of contents

WHAT MATTERS MOST IS
HOW WELL YOU
WALK THROUGH THE
FIRE

 blue beads and bones

my father and the bum

my father believed in work.
he was proud to have a
job.
sometimes he didn't have a
job and then he was very
ashamed.
he'd be so ashamed that he'd
leave the house in the morning
and then come back in the evening
so the neighbors wouldn't
know.

me,
I liked the man next door:
he just sat in a chair in
his back yard and threw darts
at some circles he had painted
on the side of his garage.
in Los Angeles in 1930
he had a wisdom that
Goethe, Hegel, Kierkegaard,
Nietzsche, Freud,
Jaspers, Heidegger and
Toynbee would find hard
to deny.

legs, hips and behind

we liked the priest because once we saw him buy
an icecream cone
we were 9 years old then and when I went to
my best friend's house his mother was usually
drinking with his father
they left the screen door open and listened
to music on the radio
his mother sometimes had her dress pulled
high and her legs excited me
made me nervous and afraid but excited
somehow
by those black polished shoes and those nylons—
even though she had buck teeth and a
very plain face.

when we were ten his father shot and
killed himself with a bullet through
the head
but my best friend and his mother went on
living in that house
and I used to see his mother going
up the hill to the market with her
shopping bag and I'd walk along beside
her
quite conscious of her legs and her
hips and her behind
the way they all moved together
and she always spoke nicely to me
and her son and I went to church and
confession together
and the priest lived in a cottage
behind the church

and a fat kind lady was always there
with him
when we went to visit
and everything seemed warm and
comfortable then in
1930
because I didn't know
that there was a worldwide
depression
and that madness and sorrow and fear were
almost everywhere.

igloo

his name was Eddie and he had a
big white dog
with a curly tail
a huskie
like one of those that pulled sleighs
up near the north pole
Igloo he called him
and Eddie had a bow and arrow
and every week or two
he'd send an arrow
into the dog's side
then run into his mother's house
through the yelping
saying that Igloo had fallen on
the arrow.
that dog took quite a few arrows and
managed to
survive
but I saw what really happened and didn't
like Eddie very much.
so when I broke Eddie's leg
in a sandlot football game
that was my way of getting even
for Igloo.

his parents threatened to sue my
parents
claiming I did it on purpose because
that's what Eddie
told them.

well, nobody had any money anyhow

and when Eddie's father got a job
in San Diego
they moved away and left the
dog.
we took him in.

Igloo turned out to be rather dumb
did not respond to very much
had no life or joy in him
just stuck out his tongue
panted
slept most of the time
when he wasn't eating
and although he wiped his ass
up and down the lawn after
defecating
he usually had a large fragrant smear of
brown
under his tail

when he was run over by an
icecream truck
3 or 4 months later
and died in a stream of scarlet
I didn't feel more than the
usual amount of grief
and loss
and I was still glad that I
had managed to
break Eddie's leg.

the mice

my father caught the baby mice
they were still alive and he
flung them into the flaming
incinerator
one by one.
the flames leaped out
and I wanted to throw my father
in there
but my being 10 years old
made that
impossible.

"o.k., they're dead," he told me,
"I killed the bastards!"

"you didn't have to do that,"
I said.

"do you want them running
all over the house?
they leave droppings, they
bring disease!
what would you do with
them?"

"I'd make pets out of
them."

"pets!
what the hell's wrong with
you anyhow?"

the flame in the incinerator
was dying down.
it was all too late.
it was over.

my father had won
again.

my garden

in the sun and in the rain
and in the day and in the night

pain is a flower
pain is flowers

blooming all the time.

legs and white thighs

the 3 of us were somewhere
between 9 and 10 years old
and we would gather in the bushes
alongside the driveway about 9:30
p.m. and look under the shade
and through the curtains at Mrs. Curson's
crossed legs—always
one foot wiggling, such a fine
thin ankle!
and she usually had her skirt
above the knee
(actually above the knee!)
and then above the garter that
held the hose sometimes we could see
a glimpse of her white thigh.
how we looked and breathed and
dreamed about those perfect
white thighs!
suddenly Mr. Curson would
get up from his chair to
let the dog out and
we'd start running through strange yards
climbing 5 foot lattice fences,
falling, getting up, running for
blocks
finally getting brave again and
stopping at some hamburger stand
for a coke.
I'm sure that Mrs. Curson never
realized what her legs and white
thighs did for us
then.

Mademoiselle from Armentières

if you gotta have wars
I suppose World War One was the best.
really, you know, both sides were much more enthusiastic,
they really had something to fight for,
they really thought they had something to fight for,
it was bloody and wrong but it was Romantic,
those dirty Germans with babies stuck on the ends of their
bayonets, and so forth, and
there were lots of patriotic songs, and the women loved *both* the
    soldiers
and their money.

the Mexican war and those other wars hardly ever happened.
and the Civil War, that was just a movie.

the wars come too fast now
even the pro-war boys grow weary,
World War Two did them in,
and then Korea, that Korea,
that was dirty, nobody won
except the black marketeers,
and BAM!—then came Vietnam,
I suppose the historians will have a name and a meaning for it,
but the young wised-up first
and now the old are getting wise,
almost everybody's anti-war,
no use having a war you can't win,
right or wrong.

hell, I remember when I was a kid it
was ten or 15 years after World War One was over,
we built model planes of Spads and Fokkers,

we bought *Flying Aces* magazine at the newsstand
we knew about Baron Manfred von Richtofen
and Capt. Eddie Rickenbacker
and we fought in dream trenches with our dream rifles
and had dream
bayonet fights with the dirty
Hun...
and those movies, full of drama and excitement,
about good old World War One, where
we almost got the Kaiser, we almost kidnapped him
once,
and in the end
we finished off all those spike-helmeted bastards
forever.

the young kids now, they don't build model warplanes
nor do they dream fight in dream rice paddies,
they know it's all useless, ordinary,
just a job like
sweeping the streets or picking up the garbage,
they'd rather go watch a Western or hang out at the
mall or go to the zoo or a football game, they're
already thinking of college and automobiles and wives
and homes and barbecues, they're already trapped
in another kind of dream, another kind of war,
and I guess it won't kill them as fast, at least not
physically.

it was wrong but World War One was fun for us
it gave us Jean Harlow and James Cagney
and "Mademoiselle from Armentières, Parley-Voo?"
it gave us
long afternoons and evenings of play
(we didn't realize that many of us were soon to die in
        another war)
yes, they fooled us nicely but we were young and loved it—
the lies of our elders—

and see how it has changed—
they can't bullshit
even a kid anymore,
not about all that.

my father's big-time fling

I came home from grammar school
one day
and my mother was sitting,
crying
there was a woman there with a large nose
and my father was there.
my mother said, "come here."
I walked over and she said,
"do you love me?"
I wasn't quite sure but I told her,
"yes."
then my father said to me,
"get the hell out of here." and my mother
said, "no, Henry, stay."
"I'll kill you," I told my father.
"oh, christ," said the woman with the big nose,
"I'm getting out of here!"
"who do you love?" my mother asked my father.
my father began crying,
"I love you both,"
he said.
"I'll kill you,"
I told him again.

the woman with the big nose grabbed her
purse and ran from the house.
"Edna! wait!" screamed my father.
he ran out of the house after her.
I ran out too.
Edna got into my father's car and
began to drive it down the
street. she had the

keys. my father ran after the
car. he managed to reach in and
grab Edna's purse. but Edna
drove off
anyhow.

back in the house
my mother said to me:
"he says he loves her. did you see her
nose, Henry?"
"yes, I saw it."
"christ," said my father, "get that kid *out* of
here!"
"I'll kill you!" I told him.
he rushed toward me.
I didn't see the blow.
my ear and face burned, I was on the
floor—
and inside my head
a flash of red
and a ringing sound.
it cleared. I got up and rushed at him,
swinging. I couldn't
kill him.

a month later
somebody broke his arm in a fight
and it made me
very happy.

the bakers of 1935

my mother, father and I
walked to the market
once a week
for our government relief food:
cans of beans, cans of
weenies, cans of hash,
some potatoes, some
eggs.
we carried the supplies
in large shopping
bags.

and as we left the market
we always stopped
outside
where there was a large
window
where we could see the
bakers
kneading
the flour into the
dough.
there were 5 bakers,
large young men
and they stood at
5 large wooden tables
working very hard,
not looking up.
they flipped the dough in
the air
and all the sizes and
designs were

different.

we were always hungry
and the sight of the men
working the dough,
flipping it in the
air was a wondrous
sight, indeed.
but then, it would come time
to leave
and we would walk away
carrying our heavy
shopping bags.

"those men have jobs,"
my father would say.
he said it each time.
every time we watched
the bakers he would say
that.

"I think I've found a new way
to make the hash,"
my mother would say
each time.
or sometimes it was
the weenies.
we ate the eggs all
different ways:
fried, poached, boiled.
one of our favorites was
poached eggs on hash.
but that favorite finally
became almost impossible
to eat.
and the potatoes, we fried
them, baked them, boiled

them.
but the potatoes had a way
of not becoming as tiresome
as the hash, the eggs, the
beans.

one day, arriving home,
we placed all our foodstuffs
on the kitchen counter and
stared at them.
then we turned away.

"I'm going to hold up a
bank!" my father suddenly
said.

"oh no, Henry, please!"
said my mother,
"please don't!"

"we're going to eat some
steak, we're going to eat
steaks until they come out
of our ears!"

"but Henry, you don't have
a gun!"

"I'll hold something in my
coat, I'll pretend it's a gun!"

"I've got a water pistol,"
I said, "you can use that."

my father looked at me.
"you," he said, "SHUT UP!"

I walked outside.
I sat on the back steps.
I could hear them in there
talking but I couldn't quite make it
out.

then I could hear them again, it was
louder.

"I'll find a new way to cook every-
thing!" my mother said.

"I'm going to rob a god-damned
bank!" my father said.

"Henry, *please, please* don't!"
I heard my mother.

I got up from the steps.
walked away into the
afternoon.

the people

all people start to
come apart finally
and there it is:
just empty ashtrays in a room
or wisps of hair on a comb
in the dissolving moonlight.

it is all ash
and dry leaves
and grief gone
like an ocean liner.

when the shoes fill with blood
you know
that the shoes are dead.

true revolution
comes from true revulsion;
when things get bad enough
the kitten will kill the lion.

the statues in the church of my childhood
and the candles that burn at their feet
if I could only take these
and open their eyes
and feel their legs
and hear their clay mouths
say the true
clay
words.

the pretty girl who rented rooms

down in New Orleans
this young pretty girl
showed me a room for rent and
it was dark in there and we stood
very close
and as we stood there
she said,
"the room is $4.50 a week."
and I said,
"I usually pay $3.50."
as we stood there in the dark
I decided to pay her $4.50 because
maybe I'd see her in the hall once in a
while
and I could not understand then why
women had to be like she was
they always waited for you
to give a sign
to make the first move
or not to make the first move
and I said,
"I'll take the room," and I gave her
the money
although I could see that
the sheets were dirty and the bed
wasn't made
but I was young and a virgin,
frightened and
confused
and I gave her the money
and she closed the door behind her
and there was no toilet and no sink

and no window.
the room was damp with suicide and death
and I undressed and lay down on the bed
and I lived there a week
and I saw many other people in the hall
old drunks
people on relief
crazy people
good young people
dull old people
but I never saw her again.

finally
I moved around the corner
to a new place
for $3.50 a week
run by another female
a 75-year-old religious maniac
with bad eyes and a limp
and we didn't have any trouble
at all

and there was a sink
and a window
in the room.

too soon

this dutchman
in a Philly bar put
3 raw eggs in his
beer
before he took a
drink.

71, he was.

I was 23 and sat 3
barstools away
burning
sorrows.

I held my head in all its
tender precious
agony

and we drank
together.

"feelin' bad, kid?" he asked.

"yeh. yeh. yeh."

"kid," he said, "I've slept longer than you've
lived."

a good old man
he was

soothing

gold
and too soon
dead.

canned heat?

not that I minded but I believe that my stint
while bumming drinks from the end barstool in
Philly
was about as low on the social scale as
you could get
until one day this gentleman walked in
and sat down beside me.
now his breath really REEKED.
I had to ask him,
"what the hell have you been drinking?"
"canned heat," he said.
"canned heat?" I asked.
"yeah, it's cheaper than the crap
you're drinking, I got a whole closet full
of it."

I was a little afraid of him and he sensed
that.
"don't worry about me," he said, "I'm all right, let me
buy you a beer."
"no, no, that's all right..."
"I insist...I'll even drink one myself."

he ordered two draft beers from Jim the
bartender.

I lifted mine. "cheers!" I said.
"cheers!" he said.

"we're different," he said, "you bum drinks,
I bum money for canned heat."

"but we're both bums!"

"right," he laughed.

we drank our beers.
I had a few coins so then I bought him
one.

we sat there not saying much.
he finished his beer, then
noticed two men sitting at the middle
of the bar.
"pardon me," he said.

he walked down, stood behind
them, asked something.

"get the hell away from me!" one of the
men said loudly.

"yeah!" yelled the other man.

then Jim the bartender yelled,
"get the hell out of here!"

the man walked to the door and was
gone.

Jim walked over to me.
"I don't want you talking to that son-of-a-
bitch!" he told me.

"Jim, he seemed like a nice guy!"

"he's crazy, he drinks canned heat!"

Jim walked off and began picking up glasses

and washing them.
he seemed very angry.
the other two men looked straight ahead,
not talking.
they also seemed quite angry.

I had no idea what canned heat was,
never heard of anybody in Philly
drinking it.

I sat and waited for happier
times.

Pershing Square, Los Angeles, 1939

One orator proving there was a God
and another proving that there wasn't.
and the crazy lady with the white and yellow
hair with the big dirty blue ribbon,
the white-striped dress, the tennis shoes,
the bare dirty ankles and the big dog
with the matted hardened fur.
and there was the guitar player and
the drum player and the flute player
all about, the winos sleeping on
the lawn
and all the while the war was rushing
toward us
but somehow nobody argued about the
war
or at least I never heard them.

in the late afternoon I would go into
one of the bars on 6th street.
I was 19 but I looked 30.
I ordered scotch-and-water.
I sat in a booth and nobody bothered
me
as the war rushed toward us.
as the afternoon dipped into evening
I refused to pay for my drinks.
and demanded more.
"Give me another drink or I'll
rip this place up!"
"All right," they told me, "one
more but it's the last and don't
come back, please."

I liked being young and mean.
the world didn't make any sense
to me.

as the night darkened I'd go back
to Pershing Square
and sit on the benches and watch
and listen to the
people.
the winos on the lawn passed bottles
of muscatel and port about
as the war rushed toward
us.

I wasn't interested in the war.
I didn't have anything, I didn't want
anything.
I had my half pint of whiskey and I
nipped at it, rolled cigarettes
and waited.
I'd read half the books in the library
and had spit them out.

the war rushed toward us.
the guitar player played his guitar.
the drummer beat his drums.
and the flute player played that thing
and it rushed toward us,
the air was clear and cool.
the stars seemed just a thousand feet
away above us
and you could see the red burning tips of
cigarettes
and there were people coughing and
laughing and swearing,
and some babbled and some prayed

and many just sat there doing
nothing,
there was nothing to do,
it was 1939 and it would never be
1939 again
in Los Angeles or any place
else
and I was young and mean and
lean
and I would never be that way
again
as it rushed toward
us.

scene from 1940:

"I knew you were a bad-ass," he said.
"you sat in the back of Art class and
you never said anything.
then I saw you in that brutal fight
with the guy with the dirty yellow
hair.
I like guys like you, you're rare, you're
raw, you make your own rules!"

"get your fucking face out of mine!"
I told him.

"you see?" he said. "you see?"

he disgusted me.
I turned and walked off.

he had outwitted me:
praise was the only thing I couldn't
handle.

my big moment

I was a packer in a factory east of
Alameda street
and I was living with a bad-assed
woman.
she fucked everybody and anybody
even me.
and I didn't have the sense to
leave.
anyhow, I worked all day and we
drank all night
and when I arrived every morning
at Sunbeam Lighting Co.
I always growled the
same thing:
"don't anybody fuck with me
I'm not in the mood for it."

this one morning
sitting on the floor in the shop
there was a large triangle of steel
with a little hand grip on top of it.
I didn't know what it was.
I'd never seen anything like it before.
it didn't matter.

all the killers and bullies and
musclemen were trying to lift it.
it wouldn't move.

"hey, Hank, baby!" a worker hollered,
"try it!"

"all right," I said.

I came around my bench, walked up
to the steel triangle, stuck my hand into the
grip and yanked. nothing. it must have
weighed at least 300 pounds.

I walked back to my bench.

"whatsa matter, Hank baby?"

"been beatin' your meat, Hank baby?"

"ah shit," I said, "for CHRIST'S SAKE!"

I walked back around my bench and swooped
        down on the
object, grabbed it, lifted it a good foot,
put it down and went back to my bench
and continued packing a light fixture into a
box.

"jesus! did you see *that,* man?"

"I saw it! he *did* it!"

"let *me* lift that son of a bitch!"

he couldn't do it. they all came and
tried again. the heavy steel object wouldn't
move.

they went back to their various jobs.
at about noon a truck came in
with a crane in the back. the
crane reached down, grabbed the steel triangle
and lifted it, with much grinding, into

the truck.

for about a week after that the
blacks and Mexicans who had
never spoken to me
tried to make friends.
I was looked upon with much new
respect.

then not long after that
everybody seemed to forget
and
I began to get verbally
sliced again
challenged again
mocked again
it was the same old
bullshit.

they knew what I knew:
that I'd never be able to do anything
like that again.

daylight saving time

I came in and all the timecards wer
e pulled so I had to go to Spindle in
personnel and he said, what happene
d, Chinaski? and I said, hell, all the t
imecards are pulled, I couldn't pun
ch in, and he said, you're an hour la
te, and I said, hell, I have 6 p.m. r
ight here on my watch, and he said, it'
s Daylight Saving Time today, and I said
, oh, and he said, how come you didn't
know it was Daylight Saving? and I sa
id, well, I don't have a TV and I don
't read the newspapers and I only lis
ten to symphony music on the radio, a
nd Spindle turned to the others in th
e office and he said, look here, Chin
aski says he doesn't have a TV and he
doesn't read newspapers and he only l
istens to symphony music on the radio
, should I really believe that? and s
omebody said, o, yes, you better beli
eve it, that cat's crazy, that cat's
crazy as they come, and Spindle got o
ut my timecard and handed it to me an
d said, all right, punch in, you'll b
e docked for the missing time, and I
took my card out to the clock and hit
it and then I walked to the work area
, all the workers snickering at me and
making sly remarks, and I handed my c
ard to supervisor Wilkins in row 88 a
nd I sat down and went to work.

the railroad yard

the feelings I get
driving past the railroad yard
(never on purpose but on my way to somewhere)
are the feelings other men have for other things.
I see the tracks and all the boxcars
the tank cars the flat cars
all of them motionless and so many of them
perfectly lined up and not an engine anywhere
(where are all the engines?).
I drive past looking sideways at it all
a wide, still railroad yard
not a human in sight
then I am past the yard
and it wasn't just the romance of it all
that gives me what I get
but something back there nameless
always making me feel better
as some men feel better looking at the open sea
or the mountains or at wild animals
or at a woman
I like those things too
especially the wild animals and the woman
but when I see those lovely old boxcars
with their faded painted lettering
and those flat cars and those fat round tankers
all lined up and waiting
I get quiet inside
I get what other men get from other things
I just feel better and it's good to feel better
whenever you can
not needing a reason.

horseshit

the horse stood in the yard and
the women went out to see the horse
and one of the women got on the horse and
rode around and almost had her head knocked off by a
tree limb and
I stood in the kitchen
measuring sunlight and wall slant and
what was willing to be measured
and one of the women was big and white and fat and
aching to be fucked
but it would take a month of talking and a year's worth of
money and I didn't have either
so I put it aside
and soon they all came back inside
and the big fat white one who was aching
sat there talking about the horse
and one of the others leaned toward me and said,
"she *iss* not available, dear!"
iss not, *iss* not. hell,
I knew that.

the light shined in and we sat there talking about
horses and waiting for her availability
and then the big fat aching one got up and walked out
and I followed and watched her mount her safe
mare
switch it—*thapp!*—
and my little switch went
            thapp!
              thapp!
and I walked back inside.

it looked like snow, damn, it looked like snow, so early,
only some of the ladies wanted it
and the others didn't want it. you know the ladies.

I went over and threw a couple of logs in the fire
and the whole thing flupped up red and
warm and we all felt
better, ready and not ready. it was Santa Fe in
October and all the poor had left town except
me.

man's best friend

I told the guy—he was watering his lawn—
you ever squirt my dog
again and you'll have to deal with me.
he just kept on watering, looking straight ahead,
and he said, I ain't worried, you punks talk about
doing it but you never do it.

he was an old white-haired guy, kind of dumb. I could
feel the dullness radiating off him.
I yanked the hose from his hand, turned him around and
sank a hard right to his gut.
he dropped like a stone and just lay on his
back on the lawn, holding his stomach and breathing
hard.
he looked pitiful.
I picked up the hose and watered him down good,
soaked his clothes, then gave him a good dose
in the face and walked off.

I went down to the store and got a fifth of scotch
and a six-pack.

when I came back he was gone.
I went up to my apartment and told Marie that I
had taken care of the matter with the guy who
squirted our dog.
she asked me, what did you do, kill him?
and I told her, no, I just explained things to him.
and she wanted to know, what did I mean, I
explained things to him?

and I told her, never mind, where are some clean

glasses?

and then the dog came walking in.
Koko.

you gotta know I liked him
plenty.

the sensitive, young poet

I never realized then what a good time I was
having
smoking cheap cigars,
in my shorts and undershirt.
proud of my barrel chest
and my biceps
and my youth, my legs,
"baby, look at my legs! ever seen legs like
that?"
prancing up and down in that hotel
room.
I was giving her a show and she just sat
there smoking
cigarettes.
she was nasty, a looker but a nasty
looker.
I knew that she would say something
vicious
but I would laugh at her.
she had seen me make a whole barfull
of men back down one
night.

each night was about the same, I'd put on
my show for her,
I'd tell her what a great brain I had.

"you're so fucking smart, what're you
doing living in a hole like this?"

"I'm just resting up, baby, I haven't
made my move yet..."

"bullshit! you're an asshole!"

"what?"

"you're an asshole!"

"why, you wasted whore, I'll rip you in half!"

then we'd go at it, swearing loudly, throwing
things, breaking things,
the phone ringing from the desk downstairs,
the other roomers banging on the walls
and me laughing, loving it,
picking up the phone, "all right, all right,
I'll keep her quiet..."

putting the phone down, looking at
her, "all right, baby, come on over here!"

"go to hell! you're disgusting!"

and I was, red-faced, cigarette
holes burnt in my undershirt,
4-day beard, yellow teeth, broken toenails,
grinning madly I'd move toward
her, glancing at the pull-down bed, I'd move
toward her saying, "hike your skirt up!
I want to see more leg!"

I was one bad dude.
she stayed 3 years then I moved on to the
next
one.

the first one never lived with another
man again.
I cured her of
that.

hunger

I have been hungry many times
but the particular time that I
think of now
was in New York City,
the night was beginning
and I was standing before the
plate glass window of a
restaurant.
and in that window
was a roasted pig,
eyeless,
with an apple in its mouth.
poor damned pig.
poor damned me.
beyond the pig
inside there
were people
sitting at tables
talking, eating, drinking.
I was not one of those people.
I felt a kinship with the pig.
we had been caught in the wrong
place
at the wrong
time.
I imagined myself in the window,
eyeless, roasted, the apple in my
mouth.
that would bring a crowd.
"hey, not much rump on him!"
"his arms are too thin!"
"I can see his ribs!"

I walked away from the window.
I walked to my room.
I still had a room.
as I walked to my room
I began to conjecture:
could I eat some paper?
some newspaper?
roaches?
maybe I could catch a rat?
a raw rat.
peel off the fur,
remove the intestines.
remove the eyes.
forego the head, the tail.

no, I'd die of
some horrible rat disease!

I walked along.
I was so hungry that everything
looked eatable:
people, fireplugs, asphalt,
wristwatches...
my belt, my shirt.

I entered the building and
walked up the stairway to my
room.

I sat in a chair.
I didn't turn on the light.
I sat there and wondered if I
was crazy
because I wasn't doing anything
to help myself.

the hunger stopped then
and I just sat there.
then I heard it:
two people in the next room,
copulating.
I could hear the bedsprings
and the moans.

I got up, walked out of the
room and back into the
street.
but I walked in a different
direction this time,
I walked away from the pig
in the window.
but I thought about the pig
and I decided that I'd die first
rather than eat that
pig.

it began to rain.
I looked up.
I opened my mouth and let in the rain
drops ... soup from the sky ...

"hey, look at that guy!"
I heard someone say.

stupid sons-of-bitches, I thought,
stupid sons-of-
bitches!

I closed my mouth and kept
walking.

the first one

after she died
I met her son in her room
a very small room without sink or toilet
in a flophouse at Beverly and Vermont.
he was thinking what kind of boyfriend are you
to let her die in a place like this?
and I was thinking, what kind of a son are you?

he asked me, do you want any of her things?
no, I said.
well, he said, we'll give them to Goodwill.

he left.

there was a large bloodstain on the bottom
sheet.

the owner of the hotel walked in. she said,
I'll have to change that sheet before I can rent this
        room to
somebody else.

o.k., I said.
I left.

I walked down to the florist
and ordered a heart-shaped arrangement, large,
for the funeral.

just say on the card, I told the lady,
from your lover. no name.

no name?

no name.

cash or credit card?

cash.

I paid and walked out on the
boulevard and
never looked
back.

the night I saw George Raft in Vegas

I bet on #6, I try red, I stare at the women's legs and breasts,
I wonder what Chekov would do, and over in the corner three men with
blue plates sit eating the carnage of my youth, they have beards
and look very much like Russians and I pat an imaginary pistol over
my left tit and try to smile like George Raft sizing up a French tart. I play
the field, I pull out dollars like turnips from the good earth, the lights
blaze and nobody says stop.

Hank, says my whore, for Christ's sake you're losing everything except me,
and I say don't forget, baby, I'm a shipping clerk. what've I got to lose
but a ball of string?

the gentlemen in the corner who look like Russians get up, knock
their plates and cups on the floor and wipe their mouths on the tablecloth.
some belch (and one farts). they laugh evilly and leave without anyone bother-
ing them. a ribbed and moiled cat comes out of somewhere,
begins licking the plates on the floor and then jumps up on the
table and walks around like his feet are wet.

I try black. the croupier's eyes dart like beetles. he makes futile
almost habitual movements to brush them away.

I switch back to red. I look around for George Raft and spill my drink

63

against my chest. Hank, says my whore, let's get out of here!
    well, at least,
I say, I ought to get a blow-job out of this. you needn't get filthy,
    the whore
says. I say, baby, I was born filthy. I try #14.

DEATH COMES SLOWLY LIKE ANTS TO A FALLEN FIG.

mirrors enclose us, I say to the croupier, ignoring the scenery of
    our despair.

I slap away a filthy thing that runs across my mouth. the cat
leaps and snatches it up as it spins upon its back kicking its
thousand legs.

then George Raft walks in. hello kid, he says, back again? I place
my last few coins on the chest of a dead elephant.
the lightning flares, they are stabbing grapefruit in the backroom,
    some-
body drops a glove and the place, the whole place, goes up in
    smoke.

we walk back to the car and fall asleep.

no title

all theories
like clichés
shot to hell,
all these small faces
looking up
beautiful and believing;
I wish to weep
but sorrow is
stupid.
I wish to believe
but belief is a
graveyard.
we have narrowed it down to
the butcherknife and the
mockingbird.
wish us
luck.

too many blacks

my first wife was from Texas and we came back
to L.A. to live
she came from oil money and I came from
someplace else.
our 2nd day in town
we drove down Vermont Avenue
to get her some art supplies
and as I was tooling my eleven-year-old
Plymouth south
a black man rolled past in a nine-year-old
green Dodge:
"hey, baby," he hollered out the window,
"what's happening?"
"nothing much happenin'," I hollered
back, "I'm just trying to make
it!"

as we stopped for a signal at
Beverly Blvd.
a black man on the corner saw me
he was standing in a broad-brimmed
Stetson pulled down in front
and wearing white leather boots
and lots of gold:
"Hank, baby, where'd you find the
blonde gash?"
"she's my mark, man," I replied,
"you know how it is."
I put it into low and pulled
away.
"listen," my first wife said
nasally,

"how come you know all these *black*
guys?"
"it's easy, baby, I've worked with them
on all the gigs. like it's
natural."

she didn't answer and when we got
to the art store
she was very upset
about the brushes
the quality of the paper
the paints weren't what she
wanted
and the total selection was
unsatisfactory.

she was very unhappy
about everything.

I stood there and watched her
beautiful ass and her very long
blonde hair

then I walked over to the picture frame
section
picked up an 8-and-one-half by
eleven
stared through the space of
it
and let her
work it
out.

white dog

I went for a walk on Hollywood Boulevard.
I looked down and there was a large white dog
walking beside me.
his pace was exactly the same as mine.
we stopped at traffic signals together.
we crossed the side streets together.
a woman smiled at us.
he must have walked 8 blocks with me.
then I went into a grocery store and
when I came out he was gone.
or she was gone.
the wonderful white dog
with a trace of yellow in its fur.
the large blue eyes were gone.
the grinning mouth was gone.
the lolling tongue was gone.

things are so easily lost.
things just can't be kept forever.

I got the blues.
I got the blues.
that dog loved and
trusted me and
I let it walk away.

blue beads and bones

as the orchid dies
and the grass goes
insane, let's have one for the lost:

I met an old man
and a tired whore
in a bar
at 8:00 in the morning
across from MacArthur Park—
we were sitting over our beers
he and I and the old whore
who had slept in an unlocked car
the night before
and wore a blue necklace.
the old guy said to me:
"look at my arms. I'm all bone.
no meat on me."
and he pulled back his sleeves
and he was right—
bone with just a layer of skin
hanging like paper.
he said, "I don't eat
nothin'."
I bought him a beer and the
whore a beer.
now there, I thought, is a man
who doesn't eat
meat, he doesn't eat
vegetables. kind of a saint.
it was like a church in there
as only the truly lost
sit in bars on Tuesday mornings

at 8:00 a.m.
then the whore said, "Jesus,
if I don't score tonight I'm
finished. I'm scared, I'm really
scared. you guys can go to skid row
when things get bad. but where can a
woman go?"
we couldn't answer her.
she picked up her beer with one hand
and played with her blue beads with the
other.
I finished my beer, went to the
corner and got a *Racing Form* from Teddy the
newsboy—age 61.
"you got a hot one today?"
"no, Teddy, I gotta see the board; money
makes them run."
"I'll give you 4 bucks. bet one for
me."
I took his 4 bucks. that would buy a sandwich,
pay parking, plus 2
coffees. I got into my car, drove
off. too early for the
track. blue beads and bones. the
universe was
bent. a cop rode his bike right up
behind me. the day had really
begun.

ax and blade

arriving to applause
through Spanish doorways
hardly ever
works. eating an apple
sometimes
works.

the ax misses by a hair's breadth
and breaks the chimney of a
lady's house.
then it swings back,
cleaves you
again, there it is,
yes, there it
is
again.

how to break clear?
a .44 magnum?
a can of ale?
the museum of pain
doesn't charge admission,
it's free as skunkshit.

from the brothels of Paris
to the hardware stores of Pasadena
from balloons
to diamond mines,
from screaming to singing
from blood to paint
from paint to miracle
from miracle to damnation.

the people walk and talk
cut to pieces
pieces of people sliced like
pie
knifed and forked and
gulped
away.

I sit in a small room
listening to classical piano on the radio.
each note bites,
nips; you fall into the mirror,
come through the other
side
staring at a lightbulb.

God sits in Munich
drinking green beer. we've got to find
Him and ask Him
why.

some notes on Bach and Haydn

it is quite something to turn your radio on
low
at 4:30 in the morning
in an apartment house
and hear Haydn
while through the blinds
you can see only the black night
as beautiful and quiet
as a flower.
and with that
something to drink,
of course,
a cigarette,
and the heater going,
and Haydn going.
maybe just 35 people
in a city of millions listening
as you are listening now,
looking at the walls,
smoking quietly,
not hating anything,
not wanting anything.
existing like mercury
you listen to a dead man's music
at 4:30 in the morning,
only he is not really dead
as the smoke from your cigarette curls up,
is not really dead,
and all is magic,
this good sound
in Los Angeles.
but now a siren takes the air,

some trouble, murder, robbery, death...
but Haydn goes on
and you listen,
one of the finest mornings of your life
like some of those when you were very young
with stupid lunch pail
and sleepy eyes
riding the early bus to the railroad yards
to scrub the windows and sides of trains
with a brush and oakite
but knowing
all the while
you would take the longest gamble,
and now having taken it,
still alive,
poor but strong,
knowing Haydn at 4:30 a.m.,
the only way to know him,
the blinds down
and the black night
the cigarette
and in my hands this pen
writing in a notebook
(my typewriter at this hour would
scream like a raped bear)
and
now
somehow
knowing the way
warmly and gently
finally
as Haydn ends.
and then a voice tells me
where I can get bacon and eggs,
orange juice, toast, coffee
this very morning
for a pleasant price

and I like this man
for telling me this
after Haydn
and I want to get dressed
and go out and find the waitress
and eat bacon and eggs
and lift the coffee cup to my mouth,
but I am distracted:
the voice tells me that Bach
will be next: "Brandenburg Concerto No. 2
in F major,"
so I go into the kitchen for a
new can of beer.
may this night never see morning
as finally one night will not,
but I do suppose morning will come this day
asking its hard way—
the cars jammed on freeways,
faces as horrible as unflushed excreta,
trapped lives less than beautiful love,
and I walk out
knowing the way
cold beer can in hand
as Bach begins
and
this good night
is still everywhere.

born to lose

I was sitting in my cell
and all the guys were tattooed
BORN TO LOSE
BORN TO DIE

all of them were able to roll a cigarette
with one hand

if I mentioned Wallace Stevens or
even Pablo Neruda to them
they'd think me crazy.

I named my cellmates in my mind:
that one was Kafka
that one was Dostoevsky
that one was Blake
that one was Céline
and that one was
Mickey Spillane.

I didn't like Mickey Spillane.

sure enough that night at lights out
Mickey and I had a fight over who got the
top bunk

the way it ended neither of us got the top bunk
we both got the hole.

after I got out of solitary I made
an appointment with the warden.
I told him I was a writer

a sensitive and gifted soul
and that I wanted to work in the library.

he gave me two more days in the hole.

when I got out I worked in the shoe factory.

I worked with Van Gogh, Schopenhauer, Dante,
    Robert Frost
and Karl Marx.

they put Spillane in license plates.

Phillipe's 1950

Phillipe's is an old time
cafe off Alameda street
just a little north and east of
the main post office.
Phillipe's opens at 5 a.m.
and serves a cup of coffee
with cream and sugar
for a nickel.

in the early mornings
the bums come down off Bunker Hill,
as they say,
"with our butts wrapped
around our ears."
Los Angeles nights have a way
of getting very
cold.
"Phillipe's," they say,
"is the only place that doesn't
hassle us."

the waitresses are old
and most of the bums are
too.

come down there some
early morning.

for a nickel
you can see the most beautiful faces
in town.

in the lobby

I saw him sitting in a lobby chair
in the Patrick Hotel
dreaming of flying fish
and he said "hello friend
you're looking good.
me, I'm not so well,
they've plucked out my hair
taken my bowels
and the color in my eyes
has gone back into the sea."

I sat down and listened
to him breathe
his last.

a bit later the clerk came over
with his green eyeshade on
and then the clerk saw what I knew
but neither of us knew
what the old man knew.

the clerk stood there
almost surprised,
taken,
wondering where the old man had gone.

he began to shake like an ape
who'd had a banana taken from his hand.

and then there was a crowd
and the crowd looked at the old man
as if he were a freak

as if there was something wrong with him.

I got up and walked out of the lobby
I went outside on the sidewalk
and I walked along with the rest of them
bellies, feet, hair, eyes
everything moving and going
getting ready to go back to the beginning
or light a cigar.

and then somebody stepped on
the back of my heel
and I was angry enough to swear.

he knows us all

hell crawls through the window
without a sound
enters my room
takes off his hat
and sits down on the couch across from me.
I laugh.
then my lamp drops off the table,
I catch it just before it hits the
floor, and in doing so,
I spill my
beer. "oh shit!" I say;
when I look up again
the son-of-a-bitch
is gone—
off looking for you,
my friend?

victory!

we struck in the middle of a
simple dawn
all their ships were in the harbor
and we torched them and created a giant
sunrise
we turned our cannon on the cathedral
cut the legs off the cavalry
found the army hung-over in the barracks
pig-stabbed them out of the dream
and the women had no chance
especially the young ones
we bared them neatly
screaming
we violated them in every way
beat the soul out of them
killed some
cut the nipples off others
then we ate all the meat and drank all
the booze in town.

war was good so long
as
you won.

when we marched out
singing
there was nothing left
back there
but fire and smoke
and death
and marching over the hill
at sunrise

the flowers rewarded us
with their
beauty.

more argument

Rilke, she said, don't you love
Rilke?

no, I said, he bores me,
poets bore me, they are shits, snails, snippets of
dust in a cheap wind.

Lorca, she said, how about Lorca?

Lorca was good when he was good. he knew how to
sing, but the only reason you like him
is because he was murdered.

Shelley, then, she said, how about Shelley?

didn't he drown in a rowboat?

then how about the lovers? I forget their names...
the two Frenchmen, one killed the
other...

o great, I said, now tell me about
Oscar Wilde.

a great man, she said.

he was clever, I said, but you believe in all these things
for the wrong reason.

Van Gogh, then, she said.

there you go, I said, there you go again.

what do you mean?

I mean that what the other painters of the time said was true:
he was an average painter.

how do you know?

I know because I paid $10 to go in and see some of his
paintings. I saw that he was interesting,
honorable, but not great.

how can you say, she asked, all these things about all these
    people?

you mean, why don't I agree with you?

for a man who is almost starving to death, you talk like some
god-damned sage!

but, I said, haven't all your heroes starved?

but this is different; you dislike everything that I like.

no, I said, I just don't like the way you
like them.

I'm leaving, she said.

I could have lied to you, I said, like most
do.

you mean men lie to me?

yes, to get at what you think is holy.

you mean, it's not holy?

I don't know, but I won't lie
to make it work.

be damned with you then, she said.

good night, I said.

she really slammed that door.

I got up and turned on the radio.

there was some pianist playing that same work by
Grieg. nothing changed. nothing
ever changed.
nothing.

wind the clock

it's just a slow day moving into a slow night.
it doesn't matter what you do
everything just stays the same.
the cats sleep it off, the dogs don't
bark,
it's just a slow day moving into a slow night.
there's nothing even dying,
it's just more waiting through a slow day moving
into a slow night.
you don't even hear the water running,
the walls just stand there
and the doors don't open.
it's just a slow day moving into a slow night.
the rain has stopped,
you can't hear a siren anywhere,
your wristwatch has a dead battery,
the cigarette lighter is out of fluid,
it's just a slow day moving into a slow night,
it's just more waiting through a slow day moving
into a slow night
like tomorrow's never going to come
and when it does
it'll be the same damn thing.

what?

sleepy now
at 4 a.m.
I hear the siren
of a white
ambulance,
then a dog
barks
once
in this tough-boy
Christmas
morning.

she comes from somewhere

probably from the bellybutton or from the shoe under the
bed, or maybe from the mouth of the shark or from
the car crash on the avenue that leaves blood and memories
scattered on the grass.
she comes from love gone wrong under an
asphalt moon.
she comes from screams stuffed with cotton.
she comes from hands without arms
and arms without bodies
and bodies without hearts.
she comes out of cannons and shotguns and old victrolas.
she comes from parasites with blue eyes and soft voices.
she comes out from under the organ like a roach.
she keeps coming.
she's inside of sardine cans and letters.
she's under your fingernails pressing blue and flat.
she's the signpost on the barricade
smeared in brown.
she's the toy soldiers inside your head
poking their lead bayonets.
she's the first kiss and the last kiss and
the dog's guts spilling like a river.
she comes from somewhere and she never stops
coming.

me, and that
old woman:
sorrow.

lifedance

the area dividing the brain and the soul
is affected in many ways by
experience—
some lose all mind and become soul:
insane.
some lose all soul and become mind:
intellectual.
some lose both and become:
accepted.

the bells

soon after Kennedy was shot
I heard this ringing of bells
an electrically charged ringing of bells
and I thought, it can't be the church
on the corner
too many people there
hated Kennedy.

I liked him
and walked to the window
thinking, well, maybe everybody is tired of
cowardly gunmen,
maybe the Russian Orthodox Church
up the street
is saying this
with their bells?
but the sound got nearer and nearer
and approached very slowly,
and I thought, what is it?
it was coming right up to my window
and then I saw it:
a small square vehicle
powered by a tiny motor
coming 2 m.p.h.
up the street:

KNIVES SHARPENED
was scrawled in red crayon
on the plywood sides
and inside sat an old man
looking straight ahead.
the ladies did not come out with their knives

the ladies were liberated and sharpened their own
knives.
the plywood box
crept down the lonely street
and with much seeming agony
managed to turn right at Normandie Blvd.
and vanish.

my own knives were dull
and *I* was not liberated
and there certainly would be more
cowardly gunmen.

much later I thought
I could still hear the
bells.

full moon

red flower of love
cut at the stem
passion has its own
way
and hatred too.
the curtain blows open
and the sky is black
out there tonight.
across the way
a man and a woman
standing up against a darkened
wall,
the red moon
whirls,
a mouse runs along
the windowsill
changing colors.
I am alone in torn levis
and a white sweat shirt.
she's with her man now
in the shadow of that wall
and as he enters her
I draw upon my
cigarette.

everywhere, everywhere

amazing, how grimly we hold onto our
misery,
ever defensive, thwarted by
the forces.
amazing, the energy we burn
fueling our anger.
amazing, how one moment we can be
snarling like a beast, then
a few moments later,
forgetting what or
why.

not hours of this or days or
months or years of this
but decades,
lifetimes
completely used up,
given over
to the pettiest
rancor and
hatred.

finally
there is nothing here for death to
take
away.

about a trip to Spain

in New York in those days they had
a system at the track
where you bought a ticket
and tried to pick 5 winners in a row
and Harry took $1000
and went up to the window and said,
"1, 8, 3, 7, 5."
and that's the way they came in
and so he took his wife to Spain
with all that money
and his wife fell for the mayor of this little
village in Spain and fucked him
and the marriage was over
and Harry came back to Brooklyn broke
and mutilated
and he has been a little crazy ever
since, but
Harry, don't despair
for you are a genius
for who else had enough pure faith
and enough courage
to go up to the window
and against all the gods of logic
say to the man at the window:
"1, 8, 3, 7, 5"?
you did it.
yes, she got the mayor
but you're the real winner
forever.

Van Gogh

vain vanilla ladies strutting
while Van Gogh did it to
himself.

girls pulling on silk
hose
while Van Gogh did it to
himself
in the field

unkissed, and
worse.

I pass him on the street:
"how's it going, Van?"

"I dunno, man," he says
and walks on.

there is a blast of color:
one more creature
dizzy with love.

he said,
then,
I want to leave.

and they look at his paintings
and love him
now.

for that kind of love

he did the right
thing

as for the other kind of love
it never arrived.

Vallejo

it is hard to find a man
whose poems do not
finally disappoint you.

Vallejo has never disappointed
me in that way.

some say he finally starved to
death.

however
his poems about the terror of being
alone
are somehow gentle and
do not
scream.

we are all tired of most
art.
Vallejo writes as a man
and not as an
artist.
he is beyond
our understanding.

I like to think of Vallejo still
alive
and walking across a
room, I find

the sound of Cesar Vallejo's
steadfast tread

imponderable.

when the violets roar at the sun

they've got us in the cage
ruined of grace and senses
and the heart roars like a lion
at what they've done to us.

the professionals

constipated writers
squatting over their machines
on hot nights
while their wives talk on the
telephone.
while the TV plays
in the background
they squat over their machines
they light cigarettes
and hope for fame
and
beautiful young girls
or at least
something to write
about.

"yeah, Barney, he's still at the typer.
I can't disturb him.
he's working on a series of short novels for
Pinnacle magazine. his central character is some
guy he calls 'Bugblast.' I got a sunburn
today. I was reading a magazine in the yard
and I forgot how long I was out there..."

endless hot summer nights.
the blades of the fan tap and rattle
against the wire cage.
the air doesn't move.
it's hard to breathe.
the people out there expect miracles
continual miracles with
words.

the world is full of
constipated writers.
and eager readers who need plenty of new
shit.
it's depressing.

the 8 count concerto

the lid to the great jar
opens
and out tumbles a
Christ child.
I throw it to my cat
who bats it about in the
air
but he soon tires of
the lack of
response.
it is near the end of
February in a
so far
banal year.
not a damn good war
in sight anywhere.
I light an Italian cigar,
it's slim, tastes bitter.
I inhale the space between
continents,
stretch my legs.
it's moments like
this—you can feel it
happening—that you grow
transformed
partly into something
else strange and
unnameable—
so when death comes
it can only take
part of
you.

I exhale a perfect
smoke ring
as a soprano sings to me
through the radio.

each night counts for something
or else we'd all
go mad.

an afternoon in February

many of the paperboys here in L.A.
are starting to grow
beards.
this makes them look suspiciously like bad
poets.

a paper container in front of me
says:
Martin Van Buren was the 8th president
of the U.S. from 1837 to 1841,
as I spill coffee on my new
dictionary.

    the phone rings.
    it is a woman who wants to talk to me.
    can't they forget me?
    am I that good?

the lady downstairs borrows a vacuum cleaner
from the manager and cackles her thanks.
her thanks drift up to me here
and disappear as two pigeons arrive
and sit on the roof in the
wind. vacuum is spelled very strangely,
I think, as I watch the 2 pigeons on the roof.
they sit motionless in the wind, just a few small
feathers on their bodies
lifting and falling.

    the phone rings again.
    "I have just about gotten over it,
    I have just about gotten over

you."
"thank you," I say and
hang up.

it is 2 in the afternoon
I have finished my coffee and had a smoke
and now the coffee water is boiling
again. there is an original painting by
Eric Heckel
on my north wall
but there is neither joy nor sorrow here now
only the paperboys
trying to grow beards
the pigeons in the wind
and the faint sound of the vacuum cleaner.

crickets

sound of doom like an approaching
cyclone

the woman across the way
keeps scolding and
screaming

she's screaming at her child

now she's clearing her
throat

I lean forward
to get a book of matches to
light my
cigarette

then she screams again

she's beating her child

the child screams

then it's quiet

all I can hear are the
crickets
droning

planet earth: where
Christ came
and

never experienced
sex with a
woman or a
man.

the angel who pushed his wheelchair

long ago he edited a little magazine
it was up in San Francisco
during the beat era
during the reading-poetry-with-jazz experiments
and I remember him because he never returned my manuscripts
even though I wrote him many letters,
humble letters, sane letters, and, at last, violent letters;
I'm told he jumped off a roof
because a woman wouldn't love him.
no matter. when I saw him again
he was in a wheelchair and carried a wine bottle to piss in;
he wrote very delicate poetry
that I, naturally, couldn't understand;
he autographed his book for me
(which he said I wouldn't like)
and once at a party I threatened to punch him and
I was drunk and he wept and
I took pity and instead hit the next poet who walked by
on the head with his piss bottle; so,
we had an understanding after all.

he had this very thin and intense woman
pushing him about, she was his arms and legs and
maybe for a while
his heart.
it was almost commonplace
at poetry readings where he was scheduled to read
to see her swiftly rolling him in,
sometimes stopping by me, saying,
"I don't see *how* we are going to get him up on the stage!"
sometimes she did. often she did.

then *she* began writing poetry, I didn't see much of it,
but, somehow, I was glad for her.
then she injured her neck while doing her yoga
and she went on disability, and again I was glad for her,
all the poets wanted to get disability insurance
it was better than immortality.

I met her in the market one day
in the bread section, and she held my hands and
trembled all over
and I wondered if they ever had sex
those two. well, they had the muse anyhow
and she told me she was writing poetry and articles
but really more poetry, she was really writing a lot,
and that's the last I saw of her
until one night somebody told me she'd o.d.'d
and I said, no, not her
and they said, yes, her.

it was a day or so later
sometime in the afternoon
I had to go to the Los Feliz post office
to mail some dirty stories to a sex mag.
coming back
outside a church
I saw these smiling creatures
so many of them smiling
the men with beards and long hair and wearing
bluejeans
and most of the women blonde
with sunken cheeks and tiny grins,
and I thought, ah, a wedding,
a nice old-fashioned wedding,
and then I saw him on the sidewalk
in his wheelchair
tragic yet somehow calm
looking greyer, a profile like a tamed hawk,

and I knew it was her funeral,
she had really o.d.'d
and he did look tragic out there.

I *do* have feelings, you know.

maybe tonight I'll try to read his book.

the circus of death

it's there
from the beginning, to the middle, to the
end,
there from light to darkness,
there through the wasted
days and nights, through
the wasted years,
the continuance
of moving toward death.
sitting with death in your lap,
washing death out of your ears
and from between your toes,
talking to death, living with death while
living through the stained walls and the flat
tires
and the changing of the guard.
living with death in your stockings.
opening the morning blinds to death,
the circus of death,
the dancing girls of death,
the yellow teeth of death,
the cobra of death,
the deserts of death.
death like a tennis ball in the mouth of
a dog.
death while eating a candlelight dinner.
the roses of death.
death like a moth.
death like an empty shoe.
death the dentist.

through darkness and light and

laughter,
through the painting of a
masterpiece,
through the applause for the bowing
actors,
while taking
a walk through Paris,
by the broken-winged
bluebird,
while
glory
runs through your fingers as
you
pick up an orange.

through the bottom of the sky
divided into sections like a
watermelon
it
bellows
silently,
consumes names and nations,
squirrels, fleas, hogs,
dandelions,
grandmothers, babies,
statues,
philosophies,
groundhogs,
the bullfighter, the bull and
all those killers in the
stadium.

it's Plato and the murderer of a
child.
the eyes in your head.
your fingernails.

it's amazing, amazing, amazing.
we're clearly at the edge.
it's thunder in a snail's shell.
it's the red mark on the black widow.
it's the mirror without a reflection.
it's the singular viewpoint.
it's in the fog over Corpus Christi.
it's in the eye of the hen.
it's on the back of the turtle.

it's moving at the sun

as you put your shoes on for the last
time
without
knowing
it.

the man?

my daughter said this when she was 5:
HERE COMES THE MAN!
what? I said. what?
I looked all around.
HERE COMES THE MAN!
O, HERE COMES THE MAN!
I went to the window and
looked out. I checked the latch
on the door.
she came out of the kitchen
with a spoon and a piepan:
clang, clang, clang!
HERE COMES THE MAN!
HERE COMES THE MAN!
O, LOOK, SEE THE MAN!
SEE THE MAN NOW!
HERE COMES THE MAN!

she means something else,
I thought, and I clapped my hands in
rhythm and we both
marched around and
sang and
laughed. me
loudest.

Christmas poem to a man in jail

hello Bill Abbott:
I appreciate your passing around my books in
jail there, my poems and stories.
if I can lighten the load for some of those guys with
my books, fine.
but literature, you know, is difficult for the
average man to assimilate (and for the unaverage man too);
I don't like most poetry, for example,
so I write mine the way I like to read it.

poetry does seem to be getting better, more
human,
the clearing up of the language has something to
do with it. (w. c. williams came along and asked
everybody to clear up the language)
then
I came along.

but writing's one thing, life's
another, we
seem to have improved the writing a bit
but life (ours and theirs)
doesn't seem to be improving very
much.

maybe if we write well enough
and live a little better
life will improve a bit
just out of shame.
maybe the artists haven't been powerful
enough,
maybe the politicians, the generals, the judges, the
priests, the police, the pimps, the businessmen have been too
strong? I don't

like that thought
but when I look at our pale and precious artists,
past and present, it does seem
possible.

(people don't like it when I talk this way.
Chinaski, get off it, they say,
you're not that great.
but
hell, I'm not talking about being
great.)

what I'm saying is
that art hasn't improved life like it
should, maybe because it has been too
private? and despite the fact that the old poets
and the new poets and myself
all seem to have had the same or similar troubles
with:
        women
        government
        God
        love
        hate
        penury
        slavery
        insomnia
        transportation
        weather
        wives, and so
forth.

you write me now
that the man in the cell next to yours
didn't like my punctuation
the placement of my commas (especially)
and also the way I digress
in order to say something precisely.
ah, he doesn't realize the *intent*

which *is*
           to loosen up, humanize, relax,
and still make as real as possible
the word on the page. the word should be like
butter or avocados or
steak or hot biscuits, or onion rings or
whatever is really
needed. it should be almost
as if you could pick up the words and
eat them.

(there is some wise-ass somewhere
out there
who will say
if he ever reads this:
"Chinaski, if I want dinner I'll go out and
order it!")

however
an artist can wander and still maintain
essential form. Dostoevsky did it. he
usually told 3 or 4 stories on the side
while telling the one in the
center (in his novels, that is).
Bach taught us how to lay one melody down on
top of another and another melody on top of
that and
Mahler wandered more than anybody I know
and I find great meaning
in his so-called formlessness.
don't let the form-and-rule boys
like that guy in the cell next to you
put one over on you. just
hand him a copy of *Time* or *Newsweek*
and he'll be
happy.

but I'm not defending my work (to you or him)
I'm defending my right to do it in the way

that makes me feel best.
I always figure if a writer is bored with his work
the reader is going to be
bored too.

and I don't believe in
perfection, I believe in keeping the
bowels loose
so I've got to agree with my critics
when they say I write a lot of shit.

you're doing 19 and ½ years
I've been writing about 40.
we all go on with our things.
we all go on with our lives.
we all write badly at times
or live badly at times.
we all have bad days
and nights.

I ought to send that guy in the cell next to yours
The Collected Works of Robert Browning for Christmas,
that'd give him the form he's looking for
but I need the money for the track,
Santa Anita is opening on the
26th, so give him a copy of *Newsweek*
(the dead have no future, no past, no present,
they just worry about commas)
and have I placed the commas here
properly,
Abbott?

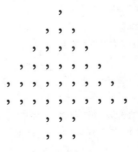

snake eyes?

it was not a good day.
there was a jagged wretchedness inhabiting
my part of the world
and now I sit at this machine
tonight
hoping for some luck and some
light
but they refuse to
fire, things refuse to
fire.
Wagner on the radio is
grand
but whatever was born in me
today
has been stamped
out, tossed
away.
I don't ask for your
sympathy
during this
Twilight of the Gods,
I am just speaking to myself
and this is the medium through
which I speak.
still, if somebody reads
this
and your day and your
night
were
akin to mine,
then somehow we've touched,
strange brother or
sister,
and we both understand that death is

not the
tragedy.
you are alone and I am
alone
and it's best that we aren't
together
comparing our pitiful
sorrows.

only let me sit before this
tired machine,
strange friend,
and write this
final
dull
line:
thank you for reading
this far.

my friends down at the corner:

dirty little bugger
about 10 years old
he sits on a box near the newsboy
he has nothing to do
but sit on that box near the newsboy
and watch
and he watches me
as I buy a newspaper
and then he runs in after me
as I go into the liquor store
and he stands there watching as I pay for a
6-pack,
dirty little bugger.
I interest him; he sickens me.
we are natural enemies.

I leave him in there.
fuck that newsboy too,
at 55 he looks like a cantaloupe.

why is it such a problem to buy
a newspaper and a few
beers?

smiling, shining, singing

my daughter looked like a young Katharine Hepburn
at the grammar school Christmas presentation.
she stood there with them
smiling, shining, singing
in the long dress I had bought for her.

she looks like Katharine Hepburn, I told her mother
who sat on my left.
she looks like Katharine Hepburn, I told my girlfriend
who sat on my right.
my daughter's grandmother was another seat away;
I didn't tell her anything.

I never did like Katharine Hepburn's acting,
but I liked the way she looked,
class, you know,
somebody you could talk to in bed for
an hour or two before going to
sleep.

I can see that my daughter is going to be a
beautiful woman.
someday when I am old
she'll probably bring the bedpan with a
kindly smile.
and she'll probably marry a truckdriver with a
heavy tread
who bowls every Thursday night
with the boys.
well, all that doesn't matter.
what matters is now.

her grandmother is a hawk of a woman.
her mother is a psychotic liberal and lover of life.
her father is an asshole.
my daughter looked like a young Katharine Hepburn.

after the Christmas presentation
we went to McDonald's and ate, and fed the sparrows.
Christmas was a week away.
we were less concerned about that than nine-tenths of the
    town.
that's class, we both have class.
to ignore Christmas takes a special wisdom
but Happy New Year to
you all.

Bruckner

listening to Bruckner now.
I relate very much to him.
he just misses
by so little.
I ache for his dead
guts.

if we all could only move it
up one notch
when necessary.
but we can't.
I remember my fight in the
rain
that Saturday night in the
alley with
Harry Tabor.
his eyes were rolling in
that great dumb
head,
one more punch
and he was mine—
I missed.

or the beautiful woman
who visited me one
night,
who sat on my couch
and told me that she was
"yours, a gift..."
but I poured whiskey,
pranced about
bragged about

myself
and finally
after returning from the
kitchen
I found her
gone.

so many near misses.
so many other near misses.

oh, Bruckner, I know!

I am listening to Bruckner
now and
I ache for his dead
guts
and for my living
soul.

we all need
something we can do well,
you know.
like scuba diving or
opening the morning
mail.

this moment

it's a farce, the great actors, the great poets, the great
statesmen, the great painters, the great composers, the
great loves,
it's a farce, a farce, a farce,
history and the recording of it,
forget it, forget it.

you must begin all over again.
throw all that out.
all of them out

you are alone with now.

look at your fingernails.
touch your nose.

begin.

the day flings itself upon
you.

one more good one

to be writing poetry at the age of 50
like a schoolboy,
surely, I must be crazy;
racetracks and booze and arguments
with the landlord;
watercolor paintings under the bed
with dirty socks;
a bathtub full of trash
and a garbage can lined with
underground newspapers;
a record player that doesn't work,
a radio that doesn't work,
and I don't work—
I sit between 2 lamps,
bottle on the floor
begging a 20-year-old typewriter
to say something, in a way and
well enough
so they won't confuse me
with the more comfortable
practitioners;
this is certainly not a game for
flyweights or Ping-Pong players—
all arguments to the contrary.

—but once you get the taste, it's good to get your
teeth into
words. I forgive those who
can't quit.
I forgive myself.
this is where the *action* is,
this is the hot horse that

comes in.
there's no grander fort
no better flag
no better woman
no better way; yet there's much else to say—
there seems as much hell in it as
magic; death gets as close as any lover has,
closer,
you know it like your right hand
like a mark on the wall
like your daughter's name,
you know it like the face on the corner
newsboy,
and you sit there with flowers and houses
with dogs and death and a boil on the neck,
you sit down and do it again and again
the machinegun chattering by the window
as the people walk by
as you sit in your undershirt,
50, on an indelicate March evening,
as their faces look in and help you write the next 5
lines,
as they walk by and say,
"the old man in the window, what's the deal with
him?"
—fucked by the muse, friends,
thank you—
and I roll a cigarette with one hand
like the old bum
I am, and then thank and curse the gods
alike,
lean forward
drag on the cigarette
think of the good fighters
like poor Hem, poor Beau Jack, poor Sugar Ray,
poor Kid Gavilan, poor Villon, poor Babe, poor
Hart Crane, poor

me, hahaha.

I lean forward,
redhot ash
falling on my wrists,
teeth into the word.
crazy at the age of 50,
I send it
home.

2

love
iz
a
big
fat
tur-
key
and
every
day
iz
thanksgiving

you do it while you're killing flies

Bach, I said, he had 20 children.
he played the horses during the day.
he fucked at night
and drank in the mornings.
he wrote music in between.

at least that's what I told her
when she asked me,
when do you do your
writing?

the 12 hour night

I found myself in middle age
working a 12 hour night,
night after night,
year after year
and somehow there seemed to be
no way out.

I was drained, empty and so
were my co-workers.
we huddled together
under the whip,
under intolerable conditions,
and many of us were
fearful of being
fired
for there was nothing left
for us.
our bodies were worn,
our spirits whipped.

there was a sense
of unreality.
one becomes so tired one
becomes so dazed,
that there is confusion and
anguish mixed in with the
deadliness.

I think that, too,
kept some of us working there.

I wasted over a decade of

12 hour nights.
I can't explain why I
remained.
cowardice, probably.

then one night I stood up
and said,
"I'm finished, I'm leaving
this job now!"

"what? what? what?"
asked my comrades.

"do you know what the
hell you're doing?"

"where will you go?"

"come back!"

"you're crazy! what will
you do?"

I walked down the rows
of them, all those faces.
I walked down the aisle
past rows and rows of
them,
all the faces looking.

"he's crazy!"

then I was in the elevator
riding down.
first floor and out.
I walked into the street,
I walked along the street,

then I turned and looked
at the towering
building, four stories high,
I saw the lights in the
windows,
I felt the presence of
those 3,000 people
in there.

then I turned and walked away
into the night.

and my life was touched by
magic.

and it still
is.

plants which easily winter kills

plants which easily winter kills,
and the hair on the eyelids of a
horse is called
brill,
and
plants which easily winter kills
are
> Campanula medium
> Digitalis purpurea
> Early-flowered Chrysanthemums
> Salvia patens
> and
> Shasta Daisy.

the United Daughters of the Confederacy was
founded in
Nashville, Tenn., Sept. 10,
1894.
the male heart weighs 10 to 12
ounces
and the female
8 to 10 ounces,
and in the 14th century
one-third of the population of England died
of the Black Death
which they say was caused by
unsanitary conditions.

and be careful of your style:
> bad: he gave all of his
>   property to
>   charity.

better:
> he gave all his property
> to
> charity.

best:
> he kept all his
> property.

the superficial area of the earth is
196,950,000 sq. miles
and the earth weighs
6,592,000,000,000,000,000,000 tons,
and my child said to me,
"thinking is not the same as
knowing."

Jesus Christ died at the age of
33 and contrary to popular belief
the sawfish does not attack
whales.

the last poetry reading

was back east.
I had a drink on the plane
and landed at the airport, 2 p.m.,
6 hours until the reading.
I was supposed to meet a lady in red,
it was 25 or 30 miles to the college.
I had a drink, scotch and water while standing up
at the bar downstairs.
then I went upstairs to another bar and had a bottle of
    imported
beer, sitting down.
when I went downstairs the lady in red was having me
paged.
she was the professor's wife and she taught high school.
the professor had a 3 o'clock class.
we drove off to a bar and waited for the professor.
she was buying and the talk was easy.
the professor came in and ordered scotch and water.
I stayed with the beer. "I've got to warble," I told them.
we drank until 7, then the professor said, "we ought to
eat," and I said, "hell, I'm not hungry, I've got to warble,
I'd rather beer up for the last hour."
they said all right and we got to the reading a little after
8.

I was lucky. after reading a couple of poems I noticed
a water pitcher and a glass sitting there
and I had a drink of water and commented upon its lack of
soul. a student walked up and gave me half-a-bottle
of good wine. I thanked him, had a drink, and went onto the
next poem. so this is how they killed Dylan Thomas? I
    thought.

well, they won't get me. I need just enough for the rent,
the beer and the horses.

I got through the reading and the next thing I knew I was in
a houseful of yuppies. they passed money for wine and we
sat around on the floor and talked. it was a
little dull but not bad.

then I was back at the professor's house
sitting up with him and sharing a 5th of whiskey.
his wife had to get up at 6:30 a.m. for her high school duties,
so just the 2 of us drank, we talked a little about literature,
but more about life and women and things that had happened.
it wasn't a bad night.
I slept on the couch downstairs.
in the morning I got up and had 2 Alka Seltzers and a coffee.
I took the professor's dog for a walk through the woods.
there were trees everywhere. those people had it made.
I came back and waited for the professor. luckily he didn't
have any classes that day.

I watched him. I knew what he was doing was wrong: a
glass of milk and a large bowl of Grapenuts. I
watched him while he ate it and listened to him in the
bathroom while he gave it back.

"what you need," I told him, "is a half-a-glass of beer in
half-a-glass of tomato juice."

"it was a good reading," he said.

"never mind the reading."

"you said you wanted to catch the 11:30 out of the
airport. I don't know if I can drive."

"I'll drive."

she had the new car and he had the old one with the stick
    shift.
it was fun learning to use the clutch again.

I stopped twice along the road while the professor
vomited. then we stopped at a gas station and had a
7-Up.

"it was a good reading."

"never mind the reading."

the professor drank 2 more 7-Ups.

"you shouldn't do that."

I waited while he vomited again.

then he suggested that we ought to have breakfast.

"breakfast?" I said. "jesus."

well, we stopped and I ordered sausage and eggs and he
ordered ham and eggs, *plus* milk and Grapenuts.

"don't eat that milk and Grapenuts," I told him.

he ate it. then I waited while he ran outside.

I ate the sausage and eggs and potatoes and toast and
drank my coffee. then I ate his ham and eggs and potatoes
and toast and drank his coffee.

I drove on to the airport, thanked him for all, and
walked into the bar. I had a tomato juice and beer. then
I had a plain beer. I just made it to the plane before it took
off. even the stewardesses didn't look as bad as

usual. I ordered a scotch and water and when the
stewardess brought it she
leaned her body all over me but didn't even
smile.

I found one of the cigars I had stolen from the professor
and leaned back and lit it with a studied flourish. I sipped
my drink and looked out the window at the clouds and the
mountains and I remembered the factories and the slaughter-
houses and the railroad track gangs, I remembered all the
dumpy 2-bit slave jobs, the low salaries, the fear, the
hatred, the despair.

so this is what killed Dylan Thomas? I thought, sipping
my drink.

bring on the next reading.

probably so

tonight
I have 2 spiders clinging to a crack in the wall
and there's one fly
loose.

a new woman lies on my bed in the next room
reading the *Herald Examiner.*

she has cooked, washed the dishes
and cleaned the tub.

she has done a good job.

I sit alone in here with the spiders
and the fly.

I hear her laugh at something in the
newspaper. she seems
happy.

I don't see how those little spiders
are ever going to get that
fly.

everybody waits
everything waits.

am I the only one
who lives like
this?

assault

bad shape. sick. can hardly hold my soul together
here in Hollywood
here on DeLongpre Ave. where the nurses live
where the experimental film makers live
where the trees live hot and sad in the sun.

here where the wheelchairs drift past
down from the home for the aged.

how long Chinaski?
how many more loves shot out of the sky?
how many more women?
how many more days and years?

pain walks through the shadows of this room.
I can feel it in my arms,
I can hear it rattling in my cheap air cooler.

I remember things and get up and walk about.
I can't stop walking
from one edge of the room to the other.

I was once a man content to be alone.
now I have been broken open,
everything has edges.

they have me—crazed and trapped.

they brought me out of myself.
they are working on me.
the onslaught is furious and relentless
and without sound.

the rivers spill over the dikes.
the sun smells like burnt cheese.
ten thousand faces on the boulevards.
I live with creatures whose existence
has nothing to do with mine.

I keep walking about this room.
I can hardly breathe.

I have given my pain a name.
I call it "Assault."

Assault, I say, will you please go out for a walk
and leave me alone?
will you please go out for a walk and
get run over by a train?

my few friends think I'm a very funny fellow.
tell me about Chinaski, they ask my girlfriend.

oh, she says, he just sits in this big chair
and moans.

they laugh.
I make people laugh.

Assault, I say, do you want something to eat?
were you once a racehorse?
why don't you
sleep?
take a rest?
die?

Assault follows me across the room
he leaps on my shoulders and shakes me.

Lorca was shot down in the road but here

in America the poets never anger anybody.
the poets don't gamble.

their poetry has the smell of clinics.
their poetry has the smell of clinics
where people die rather than live.

here they don't assassinate the poets

they don't even notice the poets.

I walk out on the street to buy a
newspaper.
Assault follows me.

we pass a beautiful young girl on the sidewalk.
I look into her eyes. she stares
back.

you can't have her, says Assault, you are an old man,
you are a crazy old man.

I'm aware of my age, I say with some dignity.

yes, and aware of death too.
you're going to die and
you don't know where you're going
but I'm coming along with you.

you rotten bastard, I say, why are you
so fond of me?

I get a newspaper and come back.
we read it together.

ah, my companion!
we bathe together, sleep together, eat

together, we
open letters together.
we write poems together.
we read poems together.

I don't know if I am Chinaski or
Assault.

some say I love my pain.

yes, I love it so much I'd like to give it to you
wrapped in a red ribbon
wrapped in a bloody red ribbon
you can have it
you can have it all.
I'll never miss it.

I'm working on getting rid of it, believe me.

I might jam it into your mailbox
or throw it into the back seat of your car.

but now
here on DeLongpre Ave.
we have just
each other.

raw with love

little dark girl with
kind eyes
when it comes time to
use the knife
I won't flinch and
I won't blame
you,
as I drive along the shore alone
as the palms wave,
the ugly heavy palms,
as the living do not arrive
as the dead do not leave,
I won't blame you,
instead
I will remember the kisses
our lips raw with love
and how you gave me
everything you had
and how I
offered you what was left of
me,
and I will remember your small room
the feel of you
the light in the window
your records
your books
our morning coffee
our noons our nights
our bodies spilled together
sleeping
the tiny flowing currents
immediate and forever

your leg my leg
your arm my arm
your smile and the warmth
of you
who made me laugh
again.
little dark girl with kind eyes
you have no
knife. the knife is
mine and I won't use it
yet.

wide and moving

it is 98 degrees and I am standing in the center
of the room in my shorts.
it is the beginning of September
and I hear the sound of high heels biting
into the pavement outside.
I walk to the window
as she comes by
in a knitted see-through pink dress,
long legs in nylon,
and the behind is
wide and moving and grand
as I stand there watching the sun run through
all that movement
and then she is gone.
all I can see is brush and lawn and pavement.
where did she come from?
and what can one do when it comes and leaves
like that?
it seems immensely unfair.
I turn around, roll myself a cigarette,
light it,
stand in front of my air cooler
and feel unjustifiably
cheated.
but I suppose she gives that same feeling to a
hundred men a day.

I decide not to mourn
and remain at the window to
watch a white pigeon
peck in the dirt
outside.

demise

the son-of-a-bitch
was one of those soft liberal guys
belly like butter who
lived in a big house, he
was a professor
and he told
her:
"he'll be your
demise."

imagine anybody saying
that: "*demise*"!

we drove in from the track,
she'd lost $57 and she said:
"we better stop for something to
drink."

she wore an old army jacket
a baseball cap
hiking boots
and when I came out with the bottle
she twisted the top off
and took a long straight swallow
a longshoreman's suicide gulp
tilting her head back behind those dark glasses.

my god, I thought.

a nice country girl like that
who loves to dance.

her 4 mad sisters will never forgive me
and that soft left-wing son-of-a-bitch
with a belly like butter (in that big
house) was
right.

the pact

"I called up Harry and his girlfriend
answered," she said. "so I asked her,
'can I speak to Harry?'
and she said, 'Harry's not here right
now.'
and I said, 'all right,
I'll phone him back.'
and Harry's girlfriend said,
'listen, I think I'd better tell you.
Harry's
dead.'"

my girlfriend and Harry used to be
lovers. Harry had a bad heart
and he couldn't get it up
anymore.

then she told me:
"Harry and I made a pact:
he said
when he died he would
come back from the dead and
let me know that there's
life after death.
I think I ought to tell you
what he's going to
try to do."

"oh really?" I said.

so each morning now when we
wake up I ask her, "well, did

Harry make it back?"

I only get worried at night.
I can see Harry's ghost bigger
than the Himalayas ripping the
bedspread off us and
standing there
with his heart and
everything else in good
order.

I've always had terrible insomnia but
at least now I have something
to wait for
besides
morning.

75 million dollars

there's Picasso
and now he's gone.
I know, it's in the papers.
there has been much about Picasso
in the papers.
we know he painted.

now there's the division of the estate.
there seem to be many little Picassos.
it will go to court, probably.
75 million dollars.

instead,
I like to think of how he worked with the brush,
doing it. wet paint, canvas, whatever.
the light. him standing there.
the process unwinding and smoking.
there's light and air and smell and the
idea, the smell of the
idea. and something to
eat. and there's a clock there.
eat the clock, Pablo. don't let the clock
eat
you.

the man leaves and his work
remains.
but to me
it's much more splendid when both
the man and the work are
here. yes, I know, I
know. 75 million dollars.

well, Picasso's gone.

immortality and fame are not always
different things. Pablo had fame,
now he has the other.

I think of old Henry Miller walking up and down
the floor in Pacific Palisades and waiting,
waiting.

we're all such good tough creative boys,
why do they let us
die?

75 million dollars.

butterflies

I believe in earning one's own way
but I also believe in the unexpected
gift
and it is a wondrous thing
when a woman who has read your works
(or parts of them, anyhow)
offers her self to you
out of the blue
a total
stranger.

such an offer
such a communion
must be taken as
holy.

the hands
the fingers
the hair
the smell
the light.

one would like to be strong enough
to turn them away

those butterflies.

I believe in earning one's own way
but I also believe in the unexpected gift.

I have no shame.

we deserve one
another

those butterflies
who flutter to my tiny
flame
and
me.

4 Christs

when I went up to Santa Cruz to read
they had the four of us
in the restaurant first
at an elevated table
with placards:
Ginsbing, Beerlinghetti, G. Cider and Chinaski.
it wasn't even the reading yet.
it was dinner first.
it looked like the Last Supper to me.
I arrived late
sat down
a thin man
with a scarf around his throat
got up and stood over me:
"guess you can't guess who I am?"
I looked.
"no."
"I'm G. Cider."
"ah, hello, Garry, I'm Chinaski."
he went back and sat
down.

Ginsbing and Beerlinghetti looked like they
were used to all the attention
we were getting.
they sat
impervious.

Jack Bitchelene hollered from the scumbag
crowd of minor poets also eating there
that night:
"hey, Chinaski, start some *shit!*"

"you *are* shit, Jack!" I hollered back,
"eat yourself and die!"
Jack loved it. he opened his dirty Brooklyn
mouth and laughed all over Santa
Cruz
his filthy grey uncombed hair
hanging in his face.
"look" I asked Beerlinghetti, "don't they
serve drinks up here
in the stratosphere?"
"we're waiting for dinner," he informed
me politely.
I got up from the table and went
over to the bar.
"give me a vodka-7," I told the
barkeep.
I got it down fast, ordered
a beer
and went back to the Last
Supper.
on the way a guy grabbed my arm:
"Ginsbing says he doesn't know how to
relate to you," he said.
I sat down at the table.
dinner came.
we ate it.
then before our transportation to the reading
arrived
we were given orders:
each was to read
20 minutes.

I read 15 minutes.
Beerlinghetti read 25 minutes.
Ginsbing read 30 minutes.
G. Cider read one hour and
12 minutes.

then it was
over.

and now the others say
I am the
Judas
among us.

$180 gone

lost my ass at the races
now sitting with the flu
listening to Wagner on the radio
I've got this small heater humming.

I'm not dead yet
yet not dead
I want to see more kneecaps under
tight nylon hose.

I'm re-grouping,
I'm dreaming up the counter-attack.

lost my ass at the races
the Sierra Madre smiling at me
lost my ass at the races
walked through a wall of defeat.

I saw a dead cat this morning
both front legs sheared off
he was lying by the garbage can
as I walked by.

this is the hardest game
defeat grows like flowers
the whores sit in chairs before their doorways
Attila the Hun sleeps in a rubber mask at night.

Wagner died, Rimbaud quit writing, Christ spit it out.

I lost my ass at the races today
and was reminded of history

of waste and of error
and of strangled dreams.

we want it too easy
and this is the hardest game.

the small heater hums
as I smoke
looking at the walls.

blue head of death

listening to Richard Strauss
is most pleasant
when you are blindfolded and up
against the wall again
facing old Spanish muskets and the
heat and the dust, the
blue head of death.
listening to Richard Strauss
reveals flashes of orange, grey and white
light,
lemonade, and cats crouched in the shade
in polarized
afternoons.

things get bad for all of
us, almost continually,
and what we do under the constant
stress
reveals
who/what we are.

Richard Strauss
is a colorful rush of craft and feeling,
he's like a loaf of french bread
cut the long way
and then loaded with all the ingredients.
it's just
right.

I leave my door open and the cats of the
neighborhood all come in. they walk over to me
and across the top of my couch

and into the bathroom, and one of them goes to
sleep on my
bed. one other sits by me and we listen
to Richard Strauss.

we're in trouble but we don't
know what to do.

young men

again and again
young men write me
the same letter:
"I can't write, but I
want to write. I
read your stuff
and I want to
write just like you.
can you
please tell me something
that will help?"

all around me the
hills are on fire,
floodwaters run
through here
swarming with
rats.
the streets roar
and yawn to
swallow me.
I'm choking
and can't breathe.

they want to write?
like me?
what do they mean?
what's writing?

I only want to go to
bed
close my eyes
and sleep
forever.

the meaning of it all

born next to cold dogs and
railroad tracks.
born to live with the
lost.

born among faces
uglier than anything
life could
devise.

born to see the 7
horse break its
leg
at 3:42 in the
afternoon.

born to lose another
woman—
clothes gone from
closet,
hairpins
lotions
lipstick
rings
left
behind.

born to dance on
one leg.

born to sit around
and watch flies

frogs
and roaches.

born to sever fingers
on the edge of
tuna cans.

born to walk about
with guts
shot out
from front to
back.

born again
and
again and
again.

guess who?

she passed from one important man
to another,
from bed to bed
from man to man
all of them
society's important men:
politicians, athletes, artists,
lawyers, doctors, entertainers,
producers, financiers,
and they all gave her one thing
or another:
gifts, money, publication,
publicity and/or
the good life.
but when she suddenly died
at 32
the only ones at her funeral
were
an aunt from Virginia
her bookie
her dope dealer
a bartender
an alcoholic neighbor
and several hired hands at the
graveyard.
but she held
2 final aces
and had the last laugh:
she'd never worked an
8 hour day
and they buried her
with all the gold
in her teeth.

I want a mermaid

speaking about going crazy
I have been thinking about
mermaids lately.
but I can't place them
properly in my
mind.
one problem that bothers
me
is where are their sexual
organs located?
do they use toilet paper?
and can they stand
on their flipper
while frying bacon and
eggs?

I think
I'd like a mermaid
to love.
sometimes in the supermarket
I see crabs and baby
octopi
and I think, well,
I could feed her that.
but how would I pack her
around at the racetrack?

I get my things and then
push my cart to the
check-out stand.
"how are you today?" she
asks.

"o.k.," I say.
she has on a
market uniform
flat shoes
earrings
a little cap
pantyhose.

she rings up my
purchases. I know
where her sexual organs
are located as
I look out the
plate glass window
and wait.

an unusual place

just thinking about
writing this poem has
already almost made me
sick
but I'll try it one more
time.

it was in Salt Lake
City
and I had the
flu
and it was cold
and I was in my
shirtsleeves.

I had given my
reading and was
ready to fly
back to L.A.

but I was with
2 girls who wanted
to make the bars

and we went into
this one place
and the girls wanted
to sit near the
front.

there was a
boy on the stage
a Japanese cowboy
and he could

holler.

I had to
make the men's room
and I ran in
there
and the urinal was
like a large shallow
bathtub
and it was
clogged and
full of urine
gently spilling across
the floor.
the entire floor
was wet
and I almost puked
into that flowing
tide of piss.

I came out and
got the girls
out of there.

that time
I didn't tip for
table service.

I'm still not
sure
which was worse—
the men's room
or that Japanese
cowboy.

that's Mormon
territory and clearly
there's work to be
done.

in this city now—

wives' heads are
battered
against kitchen
walls
by unemployed
butchers.

pimps
send out their
dreary and doped
battalions
of tired
girls.

upstairs a man
pukes
his entire stomach
into a
wastebasket.

we all drink
too much
cheap wine

search for
cigarettes

look at our
mates
across
tabletops

and wonder why
they became
ugly
so soon.

we turn our
TV's on
searching for
baseball games
soaps
and
cop
shows

but it's only
the sound
we want

some minor
distraction.

nobody cares
about
endings

we know the
end.

some of us
weaken

some of us
become
sniffers of
Christ.

some don't.

to know anything is
to score
and to score
is
necessary

that's
baseball

and that's all

the rest
of it
too.

Captain Goodwine

one goes from being a poet
to being an entertainer.
I read my stuff in Florida once
and the professor there
told me, "you realize you're
an entertainer now, don't
you?"

I began to
feel bad about that remark
because when the crowd
comes to be entertained by
you
then you become somehow
suspect.

and so, another time,
starting from Los Angeles
we took to the air and
the flight captain intro-
duced himself as
"Captain Goodwine,"
and thousands of miles
later I found myself trans-
ferred to a small 2-engine
plane and we took off and
the stewardess put a drink
in my hand
took my money and then
hollered, "drink up,
we're landing!"
we landed

took off again and she put
another drink in my hand,
took my money and then
hollered, "drink up,
we're landing!"
the 3rd time I ordered
2 drinks
although we only landed
once more.

I read twice that night in Arkansas
and ended up in a home with
clean rugs, a serving bar, a fireplace
and professors who spoke about budgets
and Fulbright scholarships, and where
the wives of the professors
sat very quietly without speaking.

they were all waiting for me
the entertainer
who had flown in with Captain
Goodwine to
entertain them to make a move on
someone's wife to break the windows
to piss on the rug to play the
fool to make them feel superior
to make them feel hip and liberated.
if I would only stick a cigarette
up the cat's ass!
if I would only take the
willing co-ed
who was doing a term paper on
Chinaski!

but I got up and went to my
poet's bedroom
closed the door

took off my clothes
went to bed and
went to sleep
thereby
entertaining myself
the best way
I knew
how.

morning love

I awakened about 10:30 a.m.
Sunday morning
and I sat straight up in bed
and I said,
"o, Jesus Christ!"
and she said,
"what's the matter, Hank?"
and I said, "it's my car. do you
remember where we parked last night?"
and she said,
"no, I don't."
and I said,
"well, I think there's something strange going on."
and I got dressed and went out on the street.
I was worried.
I had no idea where the car was
and I walked up my street and down the next
street and I didn't see it.
I have love affairs with my cars
and the older they are and/or the longer I have them
the more I care.
this one was an ancient love.
—then three blocks to the west I saw it:
parked dead center in the middle of a very narrow
street. nobody could enter the street or leave it.
my car sat there calmly like a forgotten drunk.
I walked over, got in, put the key in, and it
started.

there was no ticket.
I felt good.
I drove it to my street and parked it

carefully.

I walked back up the stairway and opened the
door.
"well, is your car all right?" she asked.
"yeah, I found it," I said, "guess where it..."
"*you worry too much about that god-damned car!*"
she snapped. "did you bring back any 7-Up, any beer?
I need something *now!*"

I undressed and got back into bed and
pushed my fat ass up against her fat
belly and never said another
word.

an old jockey

when you no longer see their name on the program
at Hollywood Park or Santa Anita
you figure they have retired
but it's not always the case.
sometimes women or bad investments
or drink or drugs
don't let them quit.
then you see them down at Caliente
on bad mounts
vying against the flashy Mexican boys
or you see them at the county fair
dashing for that first hairpin
turn.
it's like once-famous fighters
being fed to the rising small-town hero.

I was in Phoenix one afternoon
and the people were talking and chattering and talking
so I borrowed my lady's car
and got out of there
and drove to the track.
I had a fair day.
then in the last race
the jock brought in a longshot:
$48.40 and I looked at the program:
R.Y.
so that's what happened to him?
and when he pulled his mount up inside the winner's
circle he shook his whip in the air
just like he used to do at Hollywood Park.
it was like seeing the dead
newly risen:

good old R.Y.
5 pounds overweight
a bit older
and still able to
create the magic.

I hadn't noticed his name
on that $3,500 claiming race
or I would have put a small
sentimental bet on him
on his only mount of the day.

you can have your New Year's parties
your birthdays
your Christmas
your 4th of July
I'll take my kind of magic.

driving back in
I felt very good for R.Y.

when I got back they were still
chatting and talking and chatting
and my lady looked up and said,
"well, how did you do?"
and I said, "I had a lucky day."
and she said, "it's about time."

and she was right.

hard times on Carlton Way

somebody else was killed last night
as I sit looking at 12 red dying roses.
I do believe that this neighborhood must
be tougher than Spanish Harlem in N.Y.

I must get out.
I've lived here 4 years without a scratch
and in a sense my neighbors accept me.
I'm just the old guy in a white t-shirt.
but that won't help me one day.
I'm no longer broke.
I could get out of here.
I could better my living conditions.
but I have an idea
I'll never get out of here.
I like the nearby taco stand too much.
I like the cheap bars and pawn shops and
the roving insane
who sleep on our bus stop benches
or in the bushes
and raid the Goodwill container
for clothing.
I feel a bond with these
people.
I was once like them even though I
now am a published writer with some
minor success.

somebody else was killed last night
in this neighborhood
almost under my window.
I'm sentimental:

even though the roses are
almost dead
somebody brought them to me
and must I finally throw them
away?

another death last night
another death
the poor kill the poor.

I've got to get out of this
neighborhood
not for the good of my poetry
but for a reasonable chance at
old age.

as I write this
the giant who lives in the back
who wears a striped black-and-yellow
t-shirt as big as a tent
(he looks like a huge bumblebee at
six-foot-four and 290 pounds)
walks past my window and claws
the screen.

"mercy, my friend," I ask.

"there'll be no mercy," he says, turning back
to his tiny flat.

the 12 dead roses look at me.

we needed him

so big, with a cigar sticking out of his mouth
he listened patiently to the people
to the old women in the neighborhood who told him
about their arthritis and their constipation
or about the peeping toms who looked in at their
wrinkled bodies at night
breathing heavily outside the blinds.
he had patience with people
he knew something as he sat at the taco stand and
listened to the cokeheads and the meth-heads
and the ugly whores
who then listened carefully to him
he *was* the neighborhood
he was Hollywood and Western
even the pimps with their switchblades stood aside
when he walked by.

then it happened without warning: he began to get
thin. he came to my door and asked if I had some
oranges. he sat in my chair looking weak and sad,
he seemed about to cry. "I don't know what's wrong.
I can't eat. I puke it all up." I told him to go
to the doctors. he went to the Vet's Hospital, he went
to Queen of Angels, he went to Hollywood
Presbyterian. he went to other stranger places.

I went to see him the other day. he had moved out of
the neighborhood. he sat in a chair. discarded
milk cartons were on the floor, empty beef stew
cans, empty Kentucky Colonel boxes, bags of
uneaten french fries and the stale stink.

"you need a good diagnostician," I said."

"it's no use," he said.

"keep trying..."

"I've found," he said, "that I can drink buttermilk
and it stays down."

we talked some more and then I left.

now the old women ask me, "where is he? where is your
friend?"

I don't think he wants to see them.

I'll always remember him when there was trouble
around this place
running out of his apartment in back
himself large and confident
in the moonlight, long cigar in mouth
ready to right what needed to be set
right.

now it's simple and clear
that he waits as alone as a man can get.
even the devil has company, you know.
the old ladies stay inside
the taco stand has lost its lure
and when the police helicopter circles
over us in the night
and the searchlight invades our windows
illuminating the blinds it doesn't matter
like it used to matter. it's as simple
and clear as that.

Nana

she has fucked 200 men in ten
states.
5 have committed suicide
3 have gone entirely mad.
every time she moves to a new city
10 men follow her.
now she sits on my couch
in a short blue dress
and she seems
quite healthy and chipper
even looks innocent.
"I lose interest in a man,"
she says,
"as soon as he begins to care for
me."
I refill her drink
as she pulls her dress up,
shows me her black panties.
"don't these look sexy?" she asks.
I tell her that they do look sexy.
she gets up, walks across the room
through my bedroom and into the bathroom.
soon I hear the toilet flush.
her name is Nana and she has been living on
earth for the past
5,000 years.

poor Mimi

poor Mimi Trochi
she is probably the most beautiful woman I know
and young too, still young, but
she keeps running into trouble,
twice in the madhouse,
shacked up and deserted
beyond counting
but she knows I am one of those rare old-fashioned men
and she comes to me for strength
but all I can give her are hot kisses,
and we are always interrupted by lightning or chance
or bad luck
and poor Trochi and I never seem to get beyond the
hot kisses,
and I am usually luckier that way,
and she certainly must be—if you want to call it luck—
with her several children to prove it.

for one of the handsomest women on earth
this all could be a puzzle
especially since she has a mind and a soul, but
Trochi simply chooses wrong,
she chooses indifference to begin with,
she believes indifference is strength, and
I have suffered right along with Mimi Trochi and
her indifferent men and
although I have never stuck it into her
she keeps coming back
with stories and sobs
looking more handsome than ever,
we don't even kiss anymore,
all those hot kisses gone forever,

I am just not indifferent enough.
"you had your chance," she tells me,
showing me her newest baby.

I don't know what to do about it
so I phone my girlfriend and say,
"do come over. Mimi is here with her baby
and we are celebrating."
my girlfriend comes over, picks up the baby and
tortures it in her loving way
just as she does me.

and then I tell Mimi that we must leave for dinner,
my girlfriend and I,
and Mimi says, well, all the traffic
now, it's 5 in the afternoon, could I stay a while?
and so we leave handsome Mimi Trochi
there and drive off,
and I don't worry too much
because I feel that Mimi does love me in her own
way,
and coming back the next morning
I find nothing missing,
only a small phone bill later,
a call to Van Nuys and a call to Pasadena,
hardly anything for a woman in her state,
you know how it usually is:
a call to New York or Philadelphia
or London or Paris or worse.

I have her phone number written down
and I am going to invite her to my New Year's party
if she's still in town
then.
that day we left her at my place
she said she was going to try to get a job
as a belly dancer

at the Red Fez. a Turk, she said, owned the Red
Fez and he was giving her some real
trouble
but might offer her the job
anyway.

having known Mimi Trochi this long
I was afraid to ask her
what the trouble was.

a boy and his dog

there's Barry in his ripped walking shorts
he's on Thorazine
is 24
looks 38
lives with his mother in the same
apartment building
and they fight like married folk.
he wears dirty white t-shirts
and every time he gets a new dog
he names him "Brownie."
he's like an old woman really.
he'll see me getting into my Volks.
"hey, ya goin' ta work?"
"oh, no Barry, I don't work. I'm going to
the racetrack."
"yeah?"
he walks over to the car window.
"ya heard them last night?"
"who?"
"*them!* they were playin' that shit all night!
I couldn't sleep! they played until one-thirty!
didn't cha hear 'em?"
"no, but I'm in the back, Barry, you're up
front."
we live in east Hollywood among the massage parlors,
adult bookstores and the sex film theatres.
"yeah," says Barry. "I don't know what this neigh-
borhood is comin' to! ya know those other people in
        the front
unit?"
"yes."
"well, I saw through their curtains! and ya know what
they were doin'?"

"no, Barry."
"*this!*" he says and then takes his right forefinger and
pokes it against a vein in his left arm.
"really?"
"yeah! and if it ain't *that,* now we got all these
drunks in the neighborhood!"
"look, Barry, I've got to get to the racetrack."
"aw' right. but ya know what happened?"
"no, Barry."
"a cop stopped me on my Moped. and guess why?"
"speeding?"
"no! he claimed I had to have a license to drive a Moped!
that's stupid! he gave me a ticket! I almost smashed him
in the face!"
"oh yeah?"
"yeah! I almost smashed him!"
"Barry, I've got to make the first race."
"how much does it cost you to get in?"
"four dollars and twenty-five cents."
"I got into the Pomona County Fair for a dollar."
"all right, Barry."
the motor has been running. I put it into first and pull
out. in the rearview mirror I see him walk
back across the lawn.
Brownie is waiting for him,
wagging his tail.
his mother is inside waiting.
maybe Barry will slam her against the refrigerator
thinking about that cop.
or maybe they'll play checkers.
I find the Hollywood freeway
then the Pasadena freeway.
life has been tough on Barry:
he's 24
looks 38
but it all evens out finally:
he's aged a good many other people
too.

the dangerous ladies

they come visit and
sit across from me and talk
and their voices are very loud
and they laugh too much
and soon I have a headache
as they tell me about their men
how they had to throw this one out
and how the other one tried to
kill himself when they left him,
and they talk on
smiling
laughing
nodding
and most of them are a little bit
heavy and a little bit
blonde
and after they leave
I think about the men who needed them:
those are the kind of men who would consider
turning on the gas if they lost their jobs
as stock boys at
Sears-Roebuck.

those are men who need women like they once
needed their mothers.
those are men who need loud laughing
wenches of little
spiritual or physical
attraction.
and the women feast on those men
like candy
like peanuts

like sunflower seeds
and throw away the wrappers and shells
as they tell others of their womanly
conquests
while holding a warm can of Coors in one hand
and a Marlboro in the other.

sloppy love

Sally was a sloppy
leaver. she was good with farewell
notes,
she wrote them in a large
indignant hand.
Sally was always indignant, she was
good at that.

and she always took most of her
clothes,
but I'd
sit and look about—
and there'd be a pink slipper
under the bed.
I'd
get down under the bed
to get that pink slipper to
throw it in the trash
and next to the pink slipper
I'd find a pair of stained
panties.

and there were hairpins everywhere:
in the ashtray, on the dresser, in the
bathroom. and her magazines were also
everywhere with their exotic headlines:
MAN KIDNAPS GIRL, THEN
THROWS HER BODY FROM
        400 FOOT CLIFF.
9 YEAR OLD BOY RAPES
4 WOMEN IN GREYHOUND
        DEPOT RESTROOM.

Sally was a sloppy leaver.
in the top drawer next to the Kleenex
I'd find all the notes I'd written her,
neatly bound with rubber
bands.

and she was sloppy with her
photos:
I'd find one of both of us
crouched on the hood of our
'58 Plymouth—
Sally showing a lot of leg
and grinning like a Kansas City moll,
and me
showing the bottoms of my shoes
with the holes
in them.

and, there were photos of dogs,
all of them ours,
and, photos of children,
most of them
hers.

she'd leave and an
hour later
the phone would ring
and it would be
Sally
and in the background
music from a juke
box, some song I
hated, and while she talked
I'd hear men's
voices too.

"Sally, Sally," I'd say,

"come on back,
baby!"

"no," she'd say, "there are other men in the
world besides you. but
I could have loved you forever, Chinaski."

"get fucked," I'd say and hang
up.

I'd pour a drink
and while looking for a scissors in the bathroom
to trim the hair around my ears
I'd find a brassiere in one of the drawers
and hold it up to the light.

I'd drink my drink
then begin to trim the hair around my ears
deciding that I was quite a handsome man
but that I'd need to lift weights
go on a diet
get a tan,
and so forth.

after a while
the phone would ring again
and I'd lift the receiver
hang up
lift the receiver again
and let it
dangle
by the cord.

I'd trim my ear hairs, my nose hairs, my
eyebrows,
then lie down
and go to

sleep.

I'd be awakened by a sound I had never
heard before—
it felt and sounded like the warning of an
atomic attack.
I'd get up and look for the sound.
it would come from the telephone
still off the hook.
I'd
pick up the
phone.

"sir, this is the desk clerk. your phone is
off the hook."

"all right. sorry. I'll
hang up."

"don't hang up, sir. your wife is in the
elevator."

"my wife?"

"she says she's Mrs. Chinaski."

"all right, it's
possible."

"sir, can you get her out of the
elevator?
her language is abusive
and she says she won't budge
until you come and
help her ... and, sir ..."

"yes?"

"…we didn't want to call the
police…"

"yes?"

"she's laying on the floor in the
elevator, sir, and, and…she has…
urinated on
herself…"

"o.k.," I'd say and
hang up.

I'd walk out in my shorts
cigar in mouth
and press the elevator
button.
it would come up slowly:
one, two, three, four…
the doors would open
and there would be
Sally.

I'd
pick her up and
carry her out of
there.

I'd get her to the apartment
throw her on the bed
and pull off her wet
panties, skirt and stockings.
then I'd put a drink on the coffee table
nearby
sit down on the couch
and
wait.

suddenly she'd sit straight up and
look around the
room.
she'd ask
"Hank?"

"over here," I'd
wave my hand.

"oh, thank god..."

then she'd see the drink and
gulp it
down. I'd get up,
refill it, put cigarettes, an ashtray and
matches
nearby.

then she'd sit up again:
"who took my panties
off?"

"me."

"me?"

"Chinaski."

"Chinaski, you can't
fuck me."

"you pissed
yourself."

"who?"

"you..."

she'd sit straight

up then:
"Chinaski, you dance like a
queer, you dance like a
woman!"

"I'll kick your god-damned
ass!" I'd say.

then she'd put her head back on the
pillow: "I love you, Chinaski, I really
do..."

she'd start snoring then.
after a while
I'd get into bed with
her. I wouldn't want to touch her
at first. she needed a bath.
I'd get one leg up against hers;
it didn't seem too
bad. I'd try the
other.
I'd remember all the good days and the
good nights
slip one arm under her neck,
then I'd put the other around her
belly
gently.

her hair would fall back
and climb into my face.
I'd feel her inhale, then
exhale. we'd sleep like that
most of the night and into the
next afternoon. then I'd be the first to get up and
go to the bathroom
and then she'd get up and
have her turn.

winter: 44th year

I am sad
like
a
dead angel

I am sad
like
porksalt

I am mad
like
a
dead angel

a woman has
told me
when things get bad
she'll come and
bring me
lovely living
angels.

I phoned her
an hour ago
holding a
sharp knife
in my
left hand.

the phone service
said
they'd

leave the
message.

Hollywood Ranch Market

she was 32 years younger
than I was
with a body fit for the
gods.
it was 2:30 a.m.
we'd lived together for
8 months
and she shook me,
"Hank?"
"yeah?"
"I have to have some
deep fried
chicken gizzards!"
"what? again?"
"I've got to have them *now!*"
"all right."

we got up and dressed.
outside it was beginning to
rain.
we drove to the Hollywood
Ranch Market.
she ordered her
deep fried
chicken gizzards
and I ordered an ear of corn
and a roast beef
sandwich.

it was beginning to rain harder
and as we waited
a man without legs

rolled up on a little platform
he had an unforgettable face
with black eyes and
a large nose.
he grabbed my woman around
the calf of one of her
legs
with a hand the size of a
table radio:
*"hey, Cleo, baby! how ya
doin'?"*
"Beef-o!" she replied,
*"you son-of-a-bitch, how ya
doing?"*
*"great, baby, great! got a
light?"*
Beef-o had a king-size Marlboro in his
mouth.
she bent over and lit him
up as one of her breasts almost
slipped out of
her blouse.
*"you're looking great, baby,
great! who's the guy? that your
old man? hey, man, how ya doin'?"*
I bent over to shake and
my hand vanished into his.

after some more small talk
Beef-o rolled off into the
rain and she said,
"can you wait a minute?
I want to run down and see
Billy John. Billy John's just got one
arm but he's the neatest guy
you ever met! be right back!"

I paid for the orders
and stood there in the rain
holding the
bags for 10 or 15 minutes.
then Cleo came back,
"Billy John's not there, I
don't know what happened
to Billy John ..."

back in bed we sat upright
eating. I finished my corn
and my sandwich. she put her
gizzards down.
"they just don't taste right,
they just don't taste like they
used to taste."

she stretched out.
then her young lips parted
red red red with lipstick.
bits of chicken gizzard still
clung to the corners
of her mouth.
she began to
snore.

I sat and listened to the rain
then I switched out the
light.

I knew then that
I had to get out of east Hollywood!
they didn't even bother to
fix the streets
anymore.

rape

the Free Verse Poets whispered
that Julia only gave it to the
Rhyming Poets, or at least
she was always seen only with
them.

the Free Verse Poets put it into my head
to go on over there and score
one for Us.

early on that 4th of July evening
I had Julia up against the refrigerator
trapped
when this 19-year-old boy
walked into the kitchen and asked,
"hey, mom, what's going on?"

we were introduced and went into
the other room. I poured the boy
a half glass of Jack Daniels
and watched his delicate lips
pucker as he took little sips.
that would teach him not to
get in the way of his mother's
erotic life.

then there was a knock on the
door and in came Monzo the
poet and his wife
Denise. Denise hated me with
a hatred
much more powerful than

Monzo's poems.

I figured the only way to
accomplish my mission
was to drink them all senseless:
the son, Monzo, his wife and
Julia. then
I'd ravish Julia.
I had brought along enough
beer and whiskey
to accomplish this.

we drank and then the fireworks
came on at the Los Angeles
Coliseum
and by standing at the window
we could watch the show.

everybody seemed delighted.
"terribly dull shit," I said.
"Chinaski," Monzo's wife said,
"you are so negative!"

I placed my hand on Julia's ass
as we watched, I pinched her ass,
fondled the crack.
the boy was in the bathroom
vomiting.
then somebody said, "oh,
my god!"
some of the fireworks had fallen
into the tall palm trees
in the street outside
and they were burning,
one setting fire to another.

"now," I said, "there is something

that is *really* beautiful!"
"oh, Chinaski," Monzo's wife said,
"you are such an obnoxious
son-of-a-bitch!"

the fire engines came and soon spoiled
it for me. we sat down and drank some
more.
they talked. they used terms
like lower-class, middle-class, upper-
middle-class, upper-upper-class. they talked
about personal communication. they talked about the
environment and Dylan Thomas. they
discussed communes and organic gardens.
they spoke of Yoga. they talked about unstructured
schools and about growing grass
indoors with ultraviolet light. they talked
about Tim Leary, Abbie Hoffman, Jerry Rubin,
about the war in Vietnam and how they liked
certain cartoonists like Robert Crumb.
they talked about love-ins, they
talked about smoke-ins. they talked about
how everybody was fucking the American
Indian. and they drank very little while I
drank a great deal. I soon realized that
they had decided to stick it out with Julia to
keep her from being ravished.

I finally gave up
got back to my car
and drove to my place on
DeLongpre Avenue
where I uncapped a beer
lucked upon some Wagner
on the radio
and then my landlady in the back
came out and we went

over to her place
where we drank two quarts of Eastside beer
one after the other
while her old man
in a white torn undershirt
his head resting on the table
slept peacefully.
she talked about
Catholicism
(she went to mass every Sunday)
and the horrors of
hemorrhoids and gallstones
(and operations for same)
and in between we sang songs
from the 30's,
Bing Crosby songs and the like,
and when I left there at
5 a.m.
it was unclearly the 5th of July
and I had forgotten all about
my failure to ravish
Julia.

gone away

they were not quite looking at one
another nor were they trying to look
away.
they sat quietly on the uncomfortable
metal chairs in the small
glass-enclosed waiting room.
there must have been
13 or 14 of them
men and women
they looked neither
comfortable nor uncomfortable
as
I stood there
waiting for one of them
to speak
because
I didn't know which one
was the one in charge.
they were all in civilian clothes
and finally I asked:
"pardon me, but could somebody tell
me which room Betty Winters is in?"
"Betty Winters?" asked a man
dressed completely in matching brown.
I noticed he had a large ring of keys
fastened to his belt.
"yes," I answered, "I've come to
visit her. these are visiting hours,
aren't they?"
there was no answer.
the man in brown got
out of his chair. he looked at
a chart on the wall.

"Betty Winters is in 303 only she's
not there. she took restricted
leave."
the man in brown walked
back to his chair and
sat down.
the other people had remained
detached and motionless.
I almost asked, "is she coming
back?" but I already knew what
the man in brown knew:
if she didn't return she was
too insane to know she wasn't
sane enough
and if she did return she was
sane enough to know that she was
insane.

Betty Winters had asked me
to come visit her that day.
like most other afternoons
it was a wasted afternoon
for me.

as I walked back down the hall
a man ran along
in front of me. he jumped
and skipped
as he ran along
slapping at invisible marks on the
wall with his hands. he
never seemed to miss. suddenly he
let out a shout
darted into a side room and
without looking back
slammed the door
behind him.

note left on the dresser by a lady friend:

WINE: at present you are buying about 60 bottles
per month
retailing at $5 a bottle
which comes to a total of $300 a month
(plus tax).
if you can cut this down to 30 bottles a month
(one bottle per night) and buy your wine
by the case at 10% discount you will only spend
$135. the amount saved will be approx. $165 per month
or
$1980 yearly!

DINING OUT: at present you go out to eat about
4 nights a week and it costs about $25 a night, including
drinks, which comes to a total of $400 per month. cut
     your
dining out to 2 nights a week and to about $20 each
     night
(much less if you eat Chinese). this will come to
about $160 a month (plus tips). the amount saved will be
approx. $240 a month, or $2880 a year!

TELEPHONE: at present you have been spending about
     $200 per
month. this one's easy: no more long distance calls! this
will cut your expense in half. the amount saved will be
     $100 a month,
or $1200 per year.

RACETRACK: at present you are spending (losing)
     about
$90 a week. Hank, you've just got to figure out

213

a new betting system, for this comes to $360 per month!

so my dear, by cutting down on wining, dining, long
    distance
calls and losing at the track
you will save approx. $865 a month, or
get this:
$10,380 per year! REALLY!

get ready,
        get set,
            GO!

legs

Houdini was caught off guard
by a kid
who punched him in the belly
before he was ready.
he hadn't inflated his air vest
yet.
the same thing happened to me
at a party once:
I told this big guy:
"go ahead, hit me in the belly
as hard as you can! I have abs of
steel!"
just then a young girl with beautiful
legs
crossed them
and I caught a glimpse
of miraculous thigh
just as the big guy
drove his fist straight through my
stomach wall.
the pain was almost tranquil
and I couldn't see
then it got real bad
and I lifted my drink
and had some
and a while later
when I could talk
I told the big guy:
"now it's my turn!"
"yeah, right," he said and vanished into
the crowd.
the girl with the beautiful legs

left early
with somebody else.

later on that night
I drank a pint of whiskey
straight
without stopping.

there was really nothing else left
for me
to do, and I got a
well-deserved
smattering of
applause.

the artist

"look," I say, "you shouldn't have broken in
here, it's just not done..."

"why not? we waited out there for 2 hours."

"you're taking a chance of getting sliced
from gullet to asshole," I tell him.
"I often lay here in the dark
and don't want to be
bothered..."

"but I thought we were friends..."

"you shouldn't think. it's harmful."

"Hank, I haven't painted a thing this year.
I'm hurting."

"that's your dirty laundry. you're living with your
    mother.
she'll powder your
bunghole..."

"you don't like me, do you?"

"you're always talking about Art,"
I tell him. "I don't like Artists, I don't like
you, I don't like most
people, I don't like door-knockers.
I never knock on any man's door;
I expect the same."

"do you want me to leave?"

"of course."

"do you have a five?"

"I don't carry fives."

"do you have a one?"

"I don't carry ones."

"do you have any small change?"

"never carry it. holes in my pockets."

after he leaves I go into the kitchen and see where he
    and his
girlfriend broke in. she had sat through the whole
    conversation
with a 15 cent Mona Lisa smile on her
face.

I need two new hooks on
the screen. then I go and check my hunting
knife. might be better to gut him
the next time he crawls
through
there.

better for him, better for me,
better for his mother,
better for Art.

revolt in the ranks

I have just spent one-hour-and-a-half
handicapping tomorrow's
card.
when am I going to get at the poems?
well, they'll just have to wait,
they'll have to warm their feet in the
anteroom
where they'll sit gossiping about
me.
"this Chinaski, doesn't he realize that
without us he would have long ago
gone mad, been dead?"
"he knows, but he thinks he can keep
us at his beck and call!"
"he's an ingrate!"
"let's give him writer's block!"
"yeah!"
"yeah!"
"yeah!"
the little poems kick up their heels
and laugh.
then the biggest one gets up and
walks toward the door.
"hey, where you going?" he is
asked.
"somewhere where I am
appreciated."
then, he
and the others
vanish.

I open a beer, sit down at the

machine and nothing
happens.

like now.

life of the king

I awaken at 11:30 a.m.
get into my chinos and a clean green shirt
open a Miller's,
and nothing in the mailbox but the
Berkeley Tribe
which I don't subscribe to,
and on KUSC there is organ music
something by Bach
and I leave the door open
stand on the porch
walk out front
hot damn
that air is good
and the sun like golden butter on my
body. no race track today, nothing but this
beastly and magic
leisure, rolled cigarette dangling
I scratch my belly in the sun
as Paul Hindemith
rides by on a bicycle,
and down the street a lady in a
very red dress
bends down into a laundry basket
rises
hangs a sheet on a line,
bends again, rises, in all that red,
that red like snake skin
clinging moving flashing
hot damn
I keep looking, and
she sees me
pauses bent over basket

clothespin in mouth
she rises with a pair of pink
panties
smiles around the
clothespin
waves to me.
what's next? rape in the streets?
I wave back,
go in,
sit down at the machine
by the window, and now it's someone's
violin concerto in D,
and a pretty black girl in very tight pants
walking a hound,
they stop outside my window,
look in;
she has on dark shades
and her mouth opens a little, then she and the
    dog
move on.
someone might have bombed cities for this or
sold apples in the
rain.
but whoever is responsible, today I wish to
thank him
all the
way.

the silver mirror

she pulls a large silver mirror
from her purse
and starts to pencil her eyebrows.
the left eye is bruised where she
fell several nights ago.
the afternoon sun comes through the
blinds behind her.
she talks and talks as she doctors
her face: "god damn it, I'm always
falling over the strangest things...
the radiator at home, my sewing
machine, a wastebasket full of empty
tin cans..."
she lifts her drink
still gazing into the silver
mirror... "you're a funny guy, you
know that?... you say things that
nobody else would ever think of
saying... it must feel good to be
verbal that way..."
she spins the mirror in its frame
and blows cigarette smoke through it
like through a revolving door.
"I'm glad you don't like women who
wear pantyhose... it de-cunts a woman..."
the afternoon sun seeps through her
red-brown hair. quickly she crosses
her legs, swings her foot up and
down. she drops the silver mirror
back into her purse, looks up at me—
her eyes very large and the palest
green that I have ever seen, and

down through Georgia and in New Orleans
and up in Maine
the whole world is caught in her glance
and at last
the universe is
magnificent.

hunchback

moments of agony and moments of glory
march across my roof.

the cat walks by
seeming to know everything.

my luck has been better, I think,
than the luck of the cut gladiolus,
although I am not sure.

I have been loved by many women,
and for a hunchback of life,
that's lucky.

so many fingers pushing through my hair
so many arms holding me close
so many shoes thrown carelessly on my bedroom
rug.

so many searching hearts
now fixed in my memory that
I'll go to my death,
remembering.

I have been treated better than I should have
been—
not by life in general
nor by the machinery of things
but by women.

but there have been other women
who have left me

standing in the bedroom alone
doubled over—
hands holding the gut—
thinking
why why why why why why?

women go to men who are pigs
women go to men with dead souls
women go to men who fuck badly
women go to shadows of men
women go
go
because they must go
in the order of
things.

the women know better
but often chose out of
disorder and confusion.

they can heal with their touch
they can kill what they touch and
I am dying
but not dead
yet.

me and Capote

when the phone rings it's usually a man's
voice and it's like most other voices because
it usually says the same thing:
"are you Henry Chinaski, the writer?"

"I'm a sometimes writer."

"listen, I'm surprised you're listed. well,
I want to come over and talk to you, have a
few beers with you."

"why?" I ask.

"I just want to talk."

"you don't understand," I say, "there's nothing
to talk about. talking brings me down."

"but I like your writing."

"you can have that."

"I just want to come over and talk
awhile."

"I don't want to talk."

"then why are you listed?"

"I like to fuck women."

"is that why you write?"

"I'm like Truman Capote. I write to pay the rent."

I hang up.
they phone back.
I hang up.

I don't see what writing has to do with
conversation.

I also don't see what writing has to do with my
getting 3 bad books of poetry a week
in the mail.

I'm not a priest.
I'm not a guru.
I probably have more bad moments and self-
doubt than any of those who
phone me.

but when there's a knock on the door
and a creature of beauty enters
(female)
(after phoning)
hesitant
smiling
with delightful curves and magic movements
I realize
she is more dangerous than
all the armies of all time and

I know I didn't write my poems for that

and then I'm not sure
and then I don't know again

and then I forget about knowing

I get her a drink
then go into the bedroom and
take the phone off the
hook.

that's the best way to get
unlisted.

the savior: 1970

he comes by unexpectedly
long black beard and hair and barefeet
or in cheap heavy boots
and he tells me he is going to save
society from—
those bastards putting oil into the ocean
those bastards putting smoke into the sky—
and it's true
we are in a bad way
and not much is being done
and we could finally be nearing the end,
so I listen,
well, he wants to shut down the sewers.
ah, shit, man, I say, don't do that. or at least give me
30 days' notice.

well, he comes back at 2:30 in the morning
rings me out of bed. luckily there is some beer
in the refrig.
he has a better plan
he tells me.
he's going to blow up all the dams. the people will be
without water.
The Man will be forced to do
something.
he will write The Man a letter
full of his demands,
or the next dam will go,
the next city.

look, baby, don't do that.
there must be a better way of solving things,

I tell
him.

one of the brothers has deserted us, he tells
me. (the brother is suddenly more interested in
raising a child than in
saving the world).

us? he's including me?

I'm not writing another poem until
the U.S. gets out of
Vietnam, he
says.

well, to my way of looking at it, he hasn't
written a poem yet.

then I catch his eyes as I put down my beer.
I am looking at a madman.

care for another beer? I
ask.

sure, he
says.

now I haven't studied all of the dams, he says, taking a
drink of beer;
it may not be feasible in certain areas. might drown some
people. we don't want to hurt the
people.

oh, hell
no.
he hands me a mimeo pamphlet—
The American Revolution, Part II,

5 cents.

(since all this is discussed in there
I don't feel as if I were betraying a
confidence,
and I'm for saving the world
too).

we drink more beer
and I try to tell him why blowing up the dams
isn't going to
work. at least I finally get him not to shut off our
shit. but he still wants the
dams.

you can't ignore the madmen. it has been tried too
often.

have another beer,
kid.

the sun is coming up when he leaves.

he still wants the dams. he drives off in
his truck.

I open the phone book. there it is:
Sparkletts Water Co.

at 8 o'clock I am going to phone them
for a bottle to keep in the
closet.
forget my brother.
I am my own
keeper.

la femme finie

once a fine poetess
we see her photo now
and know
now
why she hasn't
written
lately.

beast

my beast comes in the afternoon
he gnaws at my gut
he paws my head
he growls
spits out part of me

my beast comes in the afternoon
while other people are taking pictures
while other people are at picnics
my beast comes in the afternoon
across a dirty kitchen floor
leering at me

while other people are employed at jobs
that stop their thinking
my beast allows me to think
about him,
about graveyards and dementia and fear
and stale flowers and decay
and the stink of ruined thunder.

my beast will not let me be
he comes to me in the afternoons
and gnaws and claws
and I tell him
as I double over, hands gripping my gut,
jesus, how will I ever explain you to
them? they think I am a coward
but they are the cowards because they refuse to
feel, their bravery is the bravery of
snails.

my beast is not interested in my unhappy
theory—he rips, chews, spits out
another piece of
me.

I walk out the door and he follows me
down the street.
we pass the lovely laughing schoolgirls
the bakery trucks
and the sun opens and closes like an oyster
swallowing my beast for a moment
as I cross at a green light
pretending that I have escaped,
pretending that I need a loaf of bread or
a newspaper,
pretending that the beast is gone forever
and that the torn parts of me are
still there
under a blue shirt and green pants
as all the faces become walls
and all the walls become impossible.

artistic selfishness

what's genius?
I don't know
but I do know that
the difference between a madman and a
professional is
that
a pro does as well as he can within what
he has set out to do
and a madman
does exceptionally well at what
he can't help
doing.

now I am looking
into this unshaded lightbulb
at 11:37 p.m. on a Monday night
thinking
tiny names
like
Van Gogh
Chatterton
Plath
Crane
Artaud

Chinaski.

my literary fly

115 degrees
not even a turkey could be happy in this heat
but it beats burning at the stake,
and like my uncle once said
(when I asked him how things were going)
he said, well, I had breakfast, I had lunch and
I think I'm going to have
dinner;
well, that's us Chinaskis,
we don't ask for much and
we don't get much,
except I have an awful good-looking girlfriend
who seems to accept my madness,
but still, it's
115 degrees.

I've got an air-cooler
a foot from my head
blowing hard
but I'm not delivering the
goods, as they say, but most people
don't like my poetry anyway.
but that's all right, because
it's 115 degrees and my girlfriend's boys
are playing outside
on their bicycles
and diving into the wading pool
while waiting to grow up.

for me,
it's too hot to fuck
too hot to paint

237

too hot to complain,
those horses across the road don't even
brush off the flies,
the flies are too tired and too hot to bite,
115 degrees,
and if I'm going to conquer the literary world
maybe we can get it down to
85 degrees first?

right now I can't write poetry,
I'm panting and lazy and ineffectual,
there's a fly on the roller of my typer
and he rides back and forth, back and forth,
my literary fly,
you son-of-a-bitch, get busy,
seek ye out another poet and bite *him*
on his ass.

I can't understand anything
except that it's hot, that's what it is,
hot, it's hot today, that's what it is, it's hot, and
that guy from Canada I drank with 3 weeks ago,
he's probably rolling in the snow right now
with Eskimo women and writing all kinds of
immortal stuff, but it's just too hot for me.

let him.

memory

I've memorized all the fish in the sea
I've memorized each opportunity strangled
and
I remember awakening one morning
and finding everything smeared with the color of
forgotten love
and I've memorized
that too.

I've memorized green rooms in
St. Louis and New Orleans
where I wept because I knew that by myself I
could not overcome
the terror of them and it.

I've memorized all the unfaithful years
(and the faithful ones too)
I've memorized each cigarette that I've rolled.
I've memorized Beethoven and New York City
I've memorized
riding up escalators, I've memorized
Chicago and cottage cheese, and the mouths of
some of the ladies and the legs of
some of the ladies
I've known
and the way the rain came down hard.
I've memorized the face of my father in his coffin,
I've memorized all the cars I have driven
and each of their sad deaths,
I've memorized each jail cell,
the face of each new president
and the faces of some of the assassins;

I've even memorized the arguments I've had with
some of the women
I've loved.

best of all
I've memorized tonight and now and the way the
light falls across my fingers,
specks and smears on the wall,
shades down behind orange curtains;
I light a rolled cigarette and then laugh a little,
yes, I've memorized it all.

the courage of my memory.

Carlton Way off Western Ave.

while the rents go up elsewhere
this is where the poor people
come to live
the people on AFDC and relief
the large families with bad jobs
the strange lonely men
on old age pensions
waiting to die.

here among the massage parlors
the pawn shops
the liquor stores
caught in the smog and the squalor
even the dogs look
inept
don't bark or
chase cats,
and the cats walk up and down the
streets
and never catch a bird
but the birds are there
but you can't see them
you only hear them
sometimes in the night
at 3:30 a.m.
after the last streetwalker has made her
last score.

the rents go up here too
but compared to most others
we are living for free
because nobody wants to live with the

likes of us.
none of us have new cars
most of us walk
and we don't care who wins the
election.

but we have wife-beaters
here too
just like the others
and child-beaters
just like the others
and sex freaks
and TV sets
just like the others

and we'll die
just like the others
only a little earlier and we'll eat
just like the others
only cheaper stuff
and lie
just like the others
only with a little less
imagination.
and even though our streetwalkers don't
look as good as your wives
I think our cats and our birds and dogs
are better
and don't forget the low
rents.

at the zoo

here's a male giraffe
he wants it
but the female's not ready
and male leans against her
he wants it
he pushes against her
follows her around
those tiny heads up in the sky
their eyes are pools of brown
the necks rock
they bump
walk about
2 ungainly forms
stretching up in the air
those stupid legs
those stupid necks

he wants it
she doesn't care
this is the way the gods have arranged it
for the moment:
one caring
one not caring

and the people watch
and throw peanuts and candy wrappers
and chunks of green and blue popsicles

they don't care either.

that's the way the gods have
arranged it
for now.

coke blues

if you think some women want only your love
try giving them some coke
they won't remember the
color of your eyes
or what you whispered in their
ear.

but lay out some lines
and give them a matchstick
(to prove they are professional)
and
unlike a woman in love
they will return
faithfully.

and one must admit
that faith in any
form
is

probably
better than the

indifference of deserted
sidewalks.

and then one
wonders
again.

nobody home

I live in this nice
place
but I'm seldom there
day or night,
all the shades down
I'm not in
there.
sometimes I think I'd like
to bake a cake
but I'm never there long enough for
the oven to get
warm.
I'm not there to answer the
phone.
I get the mail and
leave.
290 bucks rent plus
utilities.

I used to be a hermit.
a hot woman can pull a man
right out of his
shell. right out of his skin
if she wants
to.

if I ever get that cake baked
you're going to see some
fine
work.

you can see the mountains from my window

it's a block from Sunset Boulevard.
most interesting cracks in the ceiling from
the last earthquake.
and when you knock
the broken screen will sometimes fall
and dogs will run by like the Hollywood wind.
the note you leave will be read, then
forgotten.

when a hot woman meets a hermit
one of them is going to
change.

woman in the supermarket

you don't think you'll find anybody in there
at 9:30 a.m.
I was rolling my cart along and
she blocked me off with her cart between the
cheese section, the homemade pickles and the clerk
who was stamping jars of newly-arrived green
olives. I put it in reverse and
ran through the produce section, found a
good buy on navel oranges, 60 cents a pound,
picked up some cabbage and green onions, rolled
out and to the east, she was standing in front of the
Bran Flakes and the Wheaties, skirt about 3 inches
above the knee and tight-fitting. she had on a
see-through blouse with a very brief brassiere.
she had slim ankles, flat brown shoes and eyes like
a startled doe.
she smelled of cherry blossoms and French perfume.
36 years old and unhappy in marriage,
her basket was still empty. I pushed past. her eyes
were a rich mad brown. all the meats were priced too
high. I found 2 day-old spencer steaks and one
marked-down sirloin, so I took those, got a dozen medium
eggs, and there she was in the frozen vegetable section,
the mad brown eyes more unhappy than ever.
I lowered my head and pushed past and as I did she
managed to brush her rump against my flank. I got some
frozen peas, some baby limas, I rushed through the bread
    section,
decided my shopping was done, got in the checkout
line and was standing there when I felt a leg pressed
against me from ankle to waist. I stood silent smelling
the cherry blossoms and French perfume as she lit a cigarette.

I took my bags, walked to the parking lot and got into my
car, started it, backed out, turned south and
there she was standing in front of me, smiling and staring.
my car stalled as I watched
her climb into hers, hiking her skirt very high, full fat
thighs, flashes of pink panty, I got out of there fast, got
back to my kitchen, put the groceries on the table,
took the
things out of the bags and started putting them
away.

fast track

jesus christ
the horses again
I mean I said I'd never bet the horses
again
what am I doing standing out here
betting the horses?
anybody can go to the racetrack but
not everybody can
write a sonnet...

the racetrack crowd is the lowest of the breed
thinking their brains can outfox the
15 percent take.

what am I doing here?
if my publisher knew I was blowing my royalties,
if those guys in San Diego
and the one in Detroit who send me money
(a couple of fives and a ten)
or the collector in Jerome, Arizona
who paid me for some paintings,
if they knew
what would
they think?

jesus christ, I'm playing the starving poet who is
creating great Art.

I walk up to the bar with my girlfriend,
she's a handsome creature in hotpants
with long dark hair,
I order a scotch and water,

she orders a screwdriver
jesus christ
I don't have a chance
did Vallejo, Lorca and
Shelley have to go through
this?
I drink some of the scotch and
water and think,
the proper mix of the woman and the poem
is infinite Art.

then I sit down with my
Racing Form
and get back
to work.

hanging there on the wall

I used to look across the room
and think,
this female will surely do me
in
and it's not worth
it.

but I'd do nothing about it
and I wasn't
lonely.
it was more like a space to
fill in with something;
like on a canvas,
you can keep painting something on it
even if it isn't very
good.

"what are you thinking
about, you bastard?" she would
say.

"painting."

"painting? you nuts?
pour me a drink!"

and I would, and then I'd brush her
in, drink in hand, sitting
in a chair, legs crossed, kicking
her high-heeled shoes.
I'd brush her in, bad tempered,
spoiled, loud.

a painting nobody would ever
see
except me.

the hookers, the madmen and the doomed

today at the track
2 or 3 days after
the death of the
jock
came this voice
over the speaker
asking us all to stand
and observe
a few moments
of silence. well,
that's a tired
formula and
I don't like it
but I do like
silence. so we
all stood: the
hookers and the
madmen and the
doomed. I was
set to be dis-
pleased but then
I looked up at the
TV screen
and there
standing silently
in the paddock
waiting to mount
up
stood the other jocks
along with
the officials and
the trainers:

quiet and thinking
of death and the
one gone,
they stood
in a semi-circle
the brave little
men in boots and
silks,
the legions of death
appeared and
vanished, the sun
blinked once
I thought of love
with its head ripped
off
still trying to
sing and
then the announcer
said, thank you
and we all went on about
our business.

looking for Jack

like the rest of us, Jack didn't always shine too brightly:
"the whole game is run by the fags and the Jews," he'd say,
stamping up and down on my rug, grey hair hanging over hook
    nose
(he was a Jew); "look, Hank, lemme have a five ..."
walking out and around the block,
coming back, stamping on the floor,
he wanted to get the game rolling, he wanted to conquer
the world.
"damn you, Jack, I usually sleep till noon ..."
he had a little black book filled with names,
touches, contacts.
I drove him to a large place in the Hollywood hills
and he woke the guy up. the guy was good for
$20.
"they owe it to us," Jack said.
whenever he got a little ahead—that meant 40 or 50 bucks—
he'd take it to the track and lose it all,
have to walk back.
"nobody beats the horses, Hank, nobody, we're all losers, poets
are losers, who gives a damn about the poets?"
"nobody, Jack, I don't like 'em much myself ..."
he showed me early photos when he was a young man in
    Brooklyn.
he was quite handsome, quite manly, at the cutting edge of the
    Beat
movement. but the Beats died off and Jack's been crashing ever
since. when his father died he left Jack 5 or ten grand
and he got married and blew it in Spain—
his wife ended up in bed with a Spanish mayor.

Jack can still lay down the line

and when he does it well
he's still one of the best in the game
and you forget his complaining and his bumming
and his demand that a poet should get special grace.
he came out with some powerhouse poems
in a Calif. magazine
and the editor wrote me
asking where Jack was
so he could mail him contributor's copies.
well, Jack is not the suicide type
so I've been writing around and I get back
answers:
"no, he's not here, thank god."
and:
"who gives a damn?"
well, Jack's not all that bad,
especially when he forgets the bullshit and sits down to the
typer.
so if you know where he is,
write me, Henry Chinaski,
I haven't completely given up on him
even if once
in New York
he did piss on Barney Rosset's shoe
at a party.

apprentices

he used to sit in his bedroom slippers
and a silken robe
his jaw hanging open
pouches under the eyes.
they kept coming to see him
bringing wine and pills and
conversation.
the old and the young came to
see him.

he had been a very good poet
in the 30's and 40's
and maybe in the 50's.
for some reason
in the 70's he settled on
(and in)
New York
City.

it was rather like coming to see God
when you came to see
him.
and his conversation was good
especially after the wine and
pills.
he had style and grace, was
hardly
addled.
he smoked too much and the cigarettes
made him sicker than
anything. he used to spit in the paper
bag at his

feet.
he had many visitors and held his
drink well.

at the end of an evening he would select one
young female admirer to stay.
then she would
suck him off.

he's gone now.
those young admirers
never developed into the fine writer
he was. of course,
there's still time.

38,000-to-one

it was during a reading at the University of Utah.
the poets ran out of drinks
and while one was reading
2 or 3 of the others
got into a car
to drive to a liquor store
but we were blocked on the road
by the cars coming to the football stadium.
we were the only car that wanted to go the other way,
they had us: 38,000-to-one.
we sat in our lane and honked.
400 cars honked back.
the cop came over.
"look, officer," I said, "we're poets and we need a drink."
"turn around and to to the stadium," said
the officer.
"look, we need a drink. we don't want to see the
football game. we don't care who wins. we're poets, we're
reading at the Underwater Poetry Festival
at the University of Utah!"
"traffic can only move one way," said the cop,
"turn your car around and go to the stadium."
"look, I'm reading in 15 minutes. I'm Henry Chinaski!
you've heard of me, haven't you?"
"turn your car around and go to the stadium!" said the cop.
"shit," said Betsy who was at the wheel,
and she ran the car up over the curb
and we drove across the campus lawn
leaving tire marks an inch deep.
I was a bit tipsy and I don't know how long we drove
or how we got there
but suddenly we were all standing in a liquor store

and we bought wine, vodka, beer, scotch, got it and left.
we drove back,
got back there, read the ass right off that audience,
picked up our checks and left to applause.
UCLA won the football game
something to something.

a touch of steel

we had the nicest old guy
living in the back—
tall, thin, stately
with an open direct stare
and an easy smile.
his wife was squat
bow-legged,
wore black
looked down at the sidewalk
and mumbled.
she didn't comb her hair and
was usually drunk.
they'd walk past us as we sat on
the porch.
"he's a real nice old guy,"
my girlfriend would say.
"sure," I'd agree.
they had a daughter with aluminum
crutches who wore a white
nightgown and blue bathrobe
when she watered the
small brown patch
of lawn out front.

one day the daughter came out
on her crutches and started
screaming.
someone went inside and the man
had knifed his wife.

the police arrived and handcuffed
him and walked him

out to the street and
then the ambulance came and
they rolled her out
on a stretcher with wheels.

the daughter went back inside
swinging on her crutches
and closed the door.

—which proves what I've
always said:
never trust a man with
an open direct stare
and an easy smile
especially
if he smokes a pipe.

(I never saw
the nice old guy in back
smoke a pipe
but the way I see it
he must have.)

brown and solemn

the dog jumps up on the bed
crawls over me.
"are you the Word?" I ask him.
he doesn't answer.
"are you the Word? I'm looking for the Word."
he has brown and solemn eyes.
"I'm waiting for the Word," I tell him,
"I'm walking around like a man
in a large hot
frying pan."
he wags his tail and tries to
lick my face.

"listen," she says from the bathroom,
"why don't you get out of bed
and stop talking to that dog?"

my parents didn't understand me
either.

time

one collapses and surrenders
not out of choice
or lack of intelligence
or bad teeth
or bad diet

one surrenders
because that's the BEST MOVIE
around.

once I was so disgusted
with the working of things
that I dialed the time
and listened to the voice
over and over again:

"it's now 10:18 and 20 seconds
it's now 10:18 and 30 seconds..."

I didn't like the voice
and I didn't care what time it was

yet I listened.

satisfied now
I'm glad somebody stole my last watch
it was so difficult to read

satisfied now
I've got a new one

it has a black face and

white hands

and I sit there and watch
the second hand
the minute hand
the hour hand
as outside
caterpillars crawl my walls
and finally fall
like empires
like old dead loves
and new loves
fall.

night's best

with my black-faced watch
with white hands.

nobody knows the trouble I've seen

stupefied after a week's drinking and
gambling bout
I am in the tub at 10:30 in the morning
shaky
depressed
when the phone rings
and it's this young girl who sings
folk songs;
she's quit with her man
thrown his clothes out, she tells
me.
I tell her how those things work—
you're together then split
together then split
over and over
again.
yeh, she says, wanna hear my new
song? sure, I say, and she sings it to me
over the telephone.
now I am sitting on the edge of the couch
naked, wet,
listening, thinking, damn I'd like to stick it
into you, baby,
and I laugh, the song is funny,
and I say I like it, and she says,
I'm glad.
and I say, look, I've got to shape up and
make the track. keep in
touch.
I will, she says.
then I have a couple of Alka Seltzers
and an hour later

I leave, and 6 hours later
I have lost
five hundred dollars.

when I get in
I walk over to the phone
pick it up
then put it back
down.
nobody wants to hear your troubles,
I think, and that young girl doesn't want
an
old
man.

I turn on the radio
and the music is very gloomy.
I turn it off,
undress, go to the bedroom
pull down the shades and turn out all
the lights
and get into bed
and stare at the blackness,
stone cold crazy
once again.

the way it works

she came out at 9:30 a.m. in the morning
and knocked at the manager's door:
"my husband is dead!"
they went to the back of the building together
and the process began:
first the fire dept. sent two men
in dark shirts and pants
in vehicle #27
and the manager and the lady and the
two men went inside as she
sobbed.

he had knifed her last April and
had done 6 months for that.

the two men in dark shirts came out
got in their vehicle
and drove away.

then two policemen came.
then a doctor (he probably was there to
sign the death certificate).

I became tired of looking out the
window and began to
read the latest issue of
The New Yorker.

when I looked again there was a nice
sensitive-looking gray-haired gentleman
walking slowly up and down the
sidewalk in a dark suit.
then he waved in a black

hearse which
drove right up on the lawn and stopped
next to my porch.

two men got out of the hearse
opened up the back
and pulled out a gurney with 4
wheels. they rolled it to the back of the
building. when they came out again he was in a
black zipper bag and she was in
obvious distress.
they put him in the
hearse and then walked back to
her apartment and went inside
again.

I had to take out my laundry and
run some other errands.
Linda was coming to visit and
I was worried about her seeing that
hearse parked next to my porch.
so I left a note pinned to my door
that said: *Linda, don't worry.
I'm ok.* and
then I took my dirty laundry to my car and
drove away.

when I got back the hearse was gone and
Linda hadn't arrived yet.
I took the note from the door and
went inside.

well, I thought, that old guy in back
he was about my age and
we saw each other every day but
we never spoke to one another.

now we wouldn't have to.

bright lights and serpents

oftentimes I can't separate the
people from bright lights
and serpents.
in the supermarket
I see them standing and waiting
or pushing their carts.
I see rumps and ears and eyes
and skin and mouths, and
I feel curiously detached.
I suppose I fear them or
I fear their difference and
I step aside as they
pick up rolls of toilet paper,
apricots, heads of lettuce.

today I saw a man
less than 3 feet tall.
he was shorter than his
shopping basket as he
stood angrily in the aisle
looping steaks into his shopping
cart.
for a moment I felt like
touching him and saying,
"so you're different too?"
but I moved on as the
lights glared and
serpents abounded.

my total at the register
was $46.42
I paid the cashier whose

teeth kept watching me.
without warning
a bolt of lightning
flashed past my left ear
and flickered out in the fresh
egg section. then
I picked up my bag and
walked out to the parking
lot.

mean and stingy

oh, we don't give enough parties,
I just love to dance,
we never see anybody,
where have we gone lately?:
to one poetry reading.
you go to the racetrack
and you only make love to me
when you feel like it
when you're not hung over
when you're not tired from the
track.
it's the same thing over and over
again.
I'm afraid to invite people
here because you'll insult them.
you're supposed to be the greatest
poet in East Hollywood
but you're mean and stingy,
you claim we have a great relationship
you claim you like my kids,
but when I lost $75 at the track
you didn't reimburse me.
you give me very little.
we don't see anybody
it's just the same thing over and
over again,
don't you *know* that life can be
interesting? I'm so bored, bored,
bored, bored, I'm about to go
crazy!

o.k., I say, and hang up.

now she can get un-bored.
I wonder who will un-bore her
first?
probably a bore. an unemployed actor
with asthma who likes the
3 Stooges.

what she doesn't realize is
that—usually—only boring people
get bored.

and before you do
I'll hang up this
poem.

$100

the old woman with the dog
on the rope leash
asked me about the
room

her dress was shapeless,
filthy and ragged at the hem

and her dog was frightened
stunned
shocked
quivering.

I told her the landlord was
not home
and that the room was
in the back on the
2nd floor, and was
$100.

$100? she asked

yes
I
said.

she said
oh...

can I pet your
dog?
I asked.

she said
yes.

the dog would not
trust me

it ducked and pulled away and I stepped
back.

they walked away together down between the
bungalows

down the steps and
off
toward
Western
Avenue.

her dog's
eyes
were more lovely
than those of any woman I have
ever known.

this particular war

gutted:
sunk like the German navy
the Japanese fleet

gutted:
no air power
no reserves
no recourse

gutted:
as a mouse runs across the floor

gutted:
as I watch a useless blue telephone
cord
25 feet long

gutted:
again
the roads are muddied
banked with dirty snow

as everything continues:
fry-cooks
traffic signals

somebody now pounding a nail
into a wall.

gutted:
the whole thing no more than a decimal point

as she now sings her old song to her
new lover.

German bar

I had lost the last race big
somebody had stolen my coat
I could feel the flu coming on
and my tires were
low. I went in to get a
beer at the German bar
but the waitress was having a fit
her heart strangled by disappointment
grief and loss.
women get troubled all at once,
you know. I left a tip
and got out.

nobody wins.
ask Caesar.

floor job

she has a new apartment
and I stretch out on the couch
smoking
while she scrubs the floor
kneeling in her blue jeans
I see that beautiful big ass
and her long hair falls almost to the floor.
I have been in that body a few times
never enough times, of course,
but I consider my luck sufficient.

I no longer want to make her totally mine,
just my share will do
and it's a far more comfortable arrangement:
I have no need for exclusive possession.

let her have others
then she'll know who's best at heart.
otherwise she'll likely consider herself
unduly trapped.

but what a show now:
those blue jeans so tight
there's nothing so magical as a woman's ass
(unless it be some other part).

I don't want to die just yet
so now and then I look away
at a curtain or down into the
ashtray or at a dresser.

then I look back

and all the parts
are still there.

I hear soft sounds from the night outside
and I am happy.

the icecream people

the lady has me temporarily off the bottle
and now the pecker stands up
better.
however, things change overnight—
instead of listening to Shostakovitch and
Mozart through a smeared haze of smoke
the nights change, new
complexities:
we drive to Baskin-Robbins,
31 flavors:
Rocky Road, Bubble Gum, Apricot Ice, Strawberry
Cheesecake, Chocolate Mint...

we park outside and look at the icecream
people
a very healthy and satisfied people,
nary a potential suicide in sight
(they probably even vote)
and I tell her
"what if the boys saw me go in there? suppose they
find out I'm going in for a walnut peach sundae?"
"come on, chicken," she laughs and we go in
and stand with the icecream people.
none of them are cursing or threatening
the clerks.
there seem to be no hangovers or
grievances.
I am alarmed at the placid and calm wave
that flows about. I feel like a leper in a
beauty contest. we finally get our sundaes and
sit in the car and eat them.

I must admit they are quite good. a curious new
world. (all my friends tell me I am looking
better. "you're looking good, man, we thought you
were going to die there for a while...")
—those 4,500 dark nights, the jails, the
hospitals...

and later that night
there is use for the pecker, use for
love, and it is glorious,
long and true,
and afterwards we speak of easy things;
our heads by the open window with the moonlight
looking through, we sleep in each other's
arms.

the icecream people make me feel good,
inside and out.

like a cherry seed in the throat

naked in that bright
light
the four horse falls
and throws a 112 pound
boy into the hooves
of 35,000 eyes.

good night, sweet
little
motherfucker.

3

the beads swing and
the clouds obscure

the ordinary café of the world

new worlds shine in the dust
come up through the slums of the mind only
to choke on mosquito
ideas.

it's most difficult
like eating a salad
in the ordinary café of the world;
it's most difficult
to create art
here.

look about. the pieces to work with are
missing. they must be created or
found.
the critics should be generous and the critics are
seldom
generous.
they think it's easy to
put out water with fire.

but there's been no wasted effort
no matter what they've done
to us:
the critics
the lost women
the lost jobs,
damn them all anyhow
they're hardly as interesting as

this ordinary café, this ordinary world,
we know there should be a better place,

an easier place,
but there's not;
that's our secret
and it's not
much.
but it's enough.

we have chosen the ordinary,
withering fire.

to create art means
to be crazy alone
forever.

on shaving

miraculous
to grow old
through the wars & the women

rainy nights
stubbed toes
toothaches
walls
landladies
jails
hospitals
nightmares

I only shave a little
under the nose &
a touch below each
cheekbone &
the neck
under the chin

the remainder remains—
hair & man

miraculous
to grow old
through the wars & the women

that I did not become a great boxer
with much courage
does not matter
even though it was my
desire

I look at my hands shaving
my face

& my nose is too long
my cheeks sag
my teeth are my own (though I suppose
half are missing)

& I'm aware of ghosts & spirits & clouds
& blood & weeping & skeletons &
much more

it's warm tonight &
quiet while
shaving

& sometimes when I am ready to sleep &
I am upon my back
I think
yes
it's all been very
nice
      face up
                hands by side
                        gliding through the
years

miraculous
to grow old
though the wars & the women

& not to murder it by
thinking
too much about
it all

rather,

letting it all be
whatever it was/is

shaving is something like
seeing yourself in a
movie

the cup of soap takes on a
gentleness & the brush & the
mirror too

miraculous
to grow old &
shave

all the years of agony
now
seem almost
unimportant

& to shave an old face
allows the thoughts to be
steady and kind like
the electric light
above the
mirror

I hear an airplane
overhead

& there's a man flying
so high there
alone

making the sound
that comes through the ceiling and then
fades away

I listen to a dog barking
someplace in this
neighborhood & I
rinse the razor & place it behind
the mirror on the wall.

school days

I'm in bed.
it's morning
and I hear:
where are your socks?
please get dressed!
why does it take you so long to
get dressed?
where's the brush?
all right, I'll give you a head
band!
what time is it?
where's the clock?
where did you put the clock?
aren't you dressed yet?
where's the brush?
where's your sandwich?
did you make a sandwich?
I'll make your sandwich.
honey and peanut butter.
and an orange.
there.
where's the brush?
I'll use a comb.
all right, holler. you lost the brush!
where did you lose the brush?
all right. now isn't that better?
where's your coat?
go find your coat.
your coat has to be around somewhere!
listen, what are you doing?
what are you playing with?
now you've spilled it all!

I hear them open the door
go down the stairway,
get into the car.
I hear them drive away. they are gone,
down the hill
on the way to
nursery school.

neither a borrower nor a lender be

I'm at the racetrack every day
and he is too.
he used to be in the movie
industry.
I know him because somebody
I know knows him.
you know how that goes:
I really don't know him.
anyway, day after day,
he sees
me.
he yells my name.
my last name.
I'll shout a greeting
back.
once in a while there
will be a small
conversation, but not
much.

the other day
I was turning from the
window, money still
in hand, had made a
minor score, 20 win
on a horse that paid
$11.80 (that's
one hundred eighteen
dollars)
and he was
standing
there.

"how you doing?"
he asked.

"I got lucky,"
I answered.

"I haven't hit a
thing," he said,
"been dropping
between 1500 and
two thousand a
day."

"why don't you
go home?" I asked.
"lay down and take
a rest?"

he put his hand
out.
in it was a quarter
and a
dime.

"I don't have
enough for a
bet.
can you loan
me
something?
anything?"

it was the
6th race.

I hesitated,
then handed

him a
20.

"thanks, I'll see
you tomorrow."

and then he
was
gone.

although I did
see him after
the 6th race
his head was down
and he was
slowly
walking
along.

I moved off and
took a
seat.
I didn't see him
any more that
day.

or the next.
or the
next.
or the next
week.

maybe he's working
in the movie industry
again.
he's a nicer guy
than most,

I almost like
him.

or maybe he's still
at the track,
hiding out.

it's embarrassing.
I don't need the
20 that much.
they've been running
good.
and now I'm almost
afraid I'll see him
out there.
it's almost as if I was
in debt to
him.

Shakespeare had it
right.

sometimes even putting a nickel into a parking meter feels good—

precious grenades inside my skull,
I'd rather grow roses than nurture self-pity,
but sometimes it really begins to tell on me
and I have visions of house trailers and
hookers slipping into giant volcanic cracks
just south of Santa Barbara.

I guess what makes me feel better
are the truly sane: the motorcycle cop
in a clean uniform who gives me a ticket and
then rides away on two wheels like a man
who never had an itchy crotch.
or the Southern California Gas Company man
will ill-fitting dentures
who knocks on my door at 8:15 a.m. and
lights up the room with his piranha smile.

yes,
the real miracles are the thousands of tiny
people who know exactly what they are doing.

I used to look for inspiration in higher
places
but the higher you go
like to Plato or God
the less space there is in which to
stand.

check it out some day. you're driving down
the street and there's a guy hanging onto
the end of a hydraulic jack

sweat bathing his naked gut
his eyes slitted as his
body shakes and trembles
but he holds on as if to an ultimate truth, and
you smile and
you put it into second gear
check the rearview mirror and think,
yes, I can make it too, and you light a
cigarette with one hand
turn on the radio with the other
and let the good life roll along like
that.

Mahler

the phone rings and somebody says,
"hey, they made a movie about
Mahler. you ought to go see it.
he was as fucked-up as you are."

the phone rings again. it's
somebody else: "you ought to see
that Mahler movie. when you get high
you always talk about Mahler's music."

it's true: I like the way
Mahler wandered about in his
music and still retained his
passion.

he must have looked like an
earthquake walking down the
street.
he was a gambler and he shot
the works

but I'd feel foolish
walking into a movie house.
I make my own
movies.

I am the best kind of German:
in love with the music
of a great Jew.

fellow countryman

at the track
heard the voice behind me,
"Hank..."
I turned and here was this
German youth,
maybe age 34,
needed a shave, beer on his
breath.
"I know you don't like to
be bothered... but I have
this book..."

"all right, kid, look I have
to find a place..."

I took the book over to
a trash can, put it on
top, asked his name,
autographed it,
handed it back.

"I am shaking," he
said.

"it's all right," I said,
"I'm just a horseplayer."

"I've been looking for
you many days..."

"kid," I said, "listen to
me, I can't drink with you

or pal with you.
I have to leave
now."

"oh, I understand,"
he said.

that was good.
I didn't see him anymore
that day.

the next day I was
sitting alone in a small box
section.
then I heard a voice behind
me.
"hello, Hank," it said.

I didn't answer.

"who do you like in this
race?" he asked.
"I mean, out of all your
experience, who do
you like?"

I turned.
it was my friend of
yesterday.
he had another book
in his lap.
I recognized it.
it was full of photographs
and writing about one of
my trips to

Europe.

I grabbed him by the
throat, shook him a bit,
then took the book, ripped down
his pants, his shorts and
jammed the book up his
ass,
then I lifted him up over my
head,
carried him down to the
railing,
tossed him onto the
track
where the 6 horse
on post parade
stepped onto the middle of
his back.
his eyeballs
squirted out
and rolled around
looking for
Andernach
and I got up and
went to the bar
for a pretzel and a
beer.

the young man on the bus stop bench

he sits all day at the bus stop
at Sunset and Western
his sleeping bag beside him.
he's dirty.
nobody bothers him.
people leave him alone.
the police leave him alone.
he could be the 2nd coming of Christ
but I doubt it.
the soles of his shoes are completely
gone.
he just laces the tops on
and sits and watches traffic.

I remember my own youthful days
(although I traveled lighter)
they were similar:
park benches
street corners
tarpaper shacks in Georgia for
$1.25 a week
not wanting the skid row church
hand-outs
too crazy to apply for relief
daytimes spent laying in public parks
bugs in the grass biting
looking into the sky
little insects whirling above my head
the breathing of white air
just breathing and waiting.

life becomes difficult:

being ignored
and ignoring.
everything turns into white air
the head fills with white air
and as invisible women sit in rooms
with successful bright-eyed young men
conversing brilliantly about everything
your sex drive
vanishes and it really
doesn't matter.
you don't want food
you don't want shelter
you don't want anything.
sometimes you die
sometimes you don't.

as I drive past
the young man on the bus stop bench
I am comfortable in my automobile
I have money in two different banks
I own my own home
but he reminds me of my young self
and I want to help him
but I don't know what to do.

today when I drove past again
he was gone
I suppose finally the world wasn't
pleased with him being there.

the bench still sits there on the corner
advertising something.

computer class

sitting in a computer class,
first of two three-hour
sessions.
I am being sucked into the New
Age.
my wife is there too.
there are three others.
the computer-whiz-boy
whisks us through
our paces.
we each sit in front of
a computer
working our mouse,
not wanting to be
left out,
not wanting to seem
dumb,
not wanting to be
found out.
there is a desperation
in that room.
and besides, we've
paid for all
this.

"what!" says a nervous
blonde lady,
"how can I take notes?
I can't keep up!"

"take mental
notes," says

the computer-whiz-
boy.
he smiles.

the night envelops us as
we work
on.

once an impulse struck
me,
to leap up and
scream:
"shit! that's enough!
I can't handle
this!"

what stopped me
was that I knew that
it was all simple
enough,
it was only a matter
of learning the
routine.

the class actually
rolled on for an
extra hour.
at one rest break
everybody started
talking about
old television
programs which
pissed
me
off
but that finally
abated.

afterwards,
driving away in the
car
my wife asked me,
"well, did you
learn anything?"
"god, I don't know,"
I answered.

"you hungry?" she
asked.
"yeah," I said,
"we'll eat
out."

and I drove toward
the Chinese
place
and all about us
in traffic
were people who
knew about
computers or who
would soon know about
computers
and some who were
already
computed
themselves.

control panel.
find file.
select all.
show clipboard.
hide ruler.
insert header.

insert footer.
auto hyphenate.
show invisibles.
show page guides.
hide pictures.

how ya gonna keep us
down on the
farm

if
we can't find it on the
menu?

image

he sits in the chair across from me.
"you look *healthy*," he says in a voice that is
almost disappointed.

"I've given up beer and I drink only
3 bottles of white German wine each night,"
I tell him.

"are you going to let your readers know
you've reformed?" he
asks. he walks to the refrigerator and opens
the door. "all these vitamins!"

"thiamine-hcl," I say, "b-2, choline, b-6, folic
acid, zinc, e, b-12, niacin, calcium magnesium,
a-e complex, papa ... and 3 bottles of white
German wine each night."

"what's this stuff in the jars on the sink?" he
asks.

"herbs," I tell him, "goldenseal, sweet basil, alfalfa
mind, mu, lemongrass, rose hips, papaya, gotu kola, clover,
comfrey, fenugreek, sassafras and chamomile ... and I drink
    only
spring water, mineral water and my 3 bottles of white
    German
wine."

"are you going to tell your readers
about all this?"
he asks again.

"should I tell them?" I ask.
"should I tell them that I no longer
eat anything that walks on
4 legs?"

"that's what I mean," he says. "people think you are a
tough guy!"

"oh?" I say.

"and what about your *image*?" he asks. "people don't expect
you to live like this."

"I know," I say, "I've lost my beer-gut. I've come down
from a size 44 to a size 38, and I've lost 31 pounds."

"I mean," he continues, "we all thought you were a man
walking carelessly and bravely to his death, foolishly but
with style, like Don Quixote and the windmills … all that."

"we just won't tell anybody," I answer, "and maybe
we can save my
image or at least prolong it."

"you'll be turning to God next," he says.

"my god," I say, "is those 3 bottles of white German wine."

"I'm disappointed in you," he says.

"I still fuck," I reply, "and I still play the horses and I
go to the boxing matches and I still love my daughter
and I even love my present girlfriend. not that much has
changed."

"all right," he says, "we'll keep it quiet.
can you give me a ride back to my place?

my car is in the shop."

"all right," I say. "I also still drive my car."

I lock the door and we walk up the street to where I'm parked now.

the crunch (2)

too much
too little
or too late

too fat
too thin
or too bad

laughter or
tears
or immaculate
unconcern

haters
lovers

armies running through streets of pain
waving wine bottles
bayoneting and fucking everyone

or an old guy in a cheap quiet room
with a photograph of Marilyn Monroe.

there is a loneliness in this world so great
that you can see it in the slow movement of
a clock's hands.

there is a loneliness in this world so great
that you can see it in blinking neon
in Vegas, in Baltimore, in Munich.

people are tired

strafed by life
mutilated either by love or no
love.

we don't need new governments
new revolutions
we don't need new men
new women
we don't need new ways
we just need to care.

people are not good to each other
one on one.
people are just not good to each other.

we are afraid.
we think that hatred signifies
strength.
that punishment is
love.

what we need is less false education
what we need are fewer rules
fewer police
and more good teachers.

we forget the terror of one person
aching in one room
alone
unkissed
untouched
cut off
watering a plant alone
without a telephone that would never
ring
anyway.

people are not good to each other
people are not good to each other
people are not good to each other

and the beads swing and the clouds obscure
and dogs piss upon rose bushes
the killer beheads the child like taking a bite
out of an ice cream cone
while the ocean comes in and goes out
in and out
in the thrall of a senseless moon.

and people are not good to each other.

I'll send you a postcard

this guy says that for $845 I can
go to Europe and
see all the
plays and
hear all the
operas.
there's drinks on
the plane across
and good conversation
with knowledgeable
people.
I get one free
meal a day and
guided tours to
places of inter-
est.
there's even a pass
to a ski resort
and a chauffeur
is available
plus
free maps and
hand-rolled
cigars. it lasts
2 weeks.

they don't
say
anything about
getting fucked
but you get the
idea that every-
body who goes
will be.

bravo!

they applaud each work
without fail or thought
and four or five voices respond
with the same ringing
"BRAVO!" BRAVO!"
as if they had heard a fresh
and vital creative
breakthrough.

where have the audiences gone
that were able to select and
discriminate?

now the thought in the collective mind of
the audience is:
we understand
we *know*
therefore we
respond
as one.

and afterwards
at the wheels of their automobiles
they dash out of the underground
parking lot
more rude and crass
than any boxing match crowd
than any horse race crowd
cutting off others
swerving
cursing.

the *March to the Gallows*, indeed
Pictures at an Exhibition, of course
the *Bolero*, yes
The Afternoon of a Faun?

honking
zooming toward the freeways
BRAVO west L.A.
BRAVO Westwood Village
BRAVO the Hollywood Hills
BRAVO Beverly Hills.

Symphonie Pathétique, indeed.

downtown

nobody goes downtown anymore
the plants and trees have been cut away around
Pershing Square
the grass is brown
and the street preachers are not as good
as they used to be
and down on Broadway
the Latinos stand in long colorful lines
waiting to see Latino action movies.
I walk down to Clifton's cafeteria
it's still there
the waterfall is still there
the few white faces are old and poor
dignified
dressed in 1950s clothing
sitting at small tables on the first
floor.
I take my food upstairs to the
third floor—
all Latinos at the tables there
faces more tired than hostile
the men at rest from their factory jobs
their once beautiful wives now
heavy and satisfied
the men wanting badly to go out and raise hell
but now the money is needed for
clothing, tires, toys, TV sets
children's shoes, the rent.

I finish eating
walk down to the first floor and out,
and nearby is a penny arcade.

I remember it from the 1940s.
I walk in.
it is full of young Latinos and Blacks
between the ages of six and
fifteen
and they shoot machine guns
play mechanical soccer
and the piped-in salsa music is very
loud.
they fly spacecraft
test their strength
fight in the ring
have horse races
auto races
but none of them want their fortunes told.
I lean against a wall and
watch them.

I go outside again.
I walk down and across from the *Herald-
    Examiner*
building
where my car is parked.
I get in. then I drive away.
it's Sunday. and it's true
like they say: the old gang never
goes downtown anymore.

the blue pigeon

getting a car wash today
about 1:30 p.m.
I saw this blue pigeon
come floating through the
air awkwardly
it hit the asphalt
wings spread wide
and lay there shivering
one eye open
it was dying
and I walked away
and stood by my car
where
the fellows were wiping
the windows
and then a Camaro
came fast and
got the pigeon.
turned it into a red stain
and one of the fellows
said, "Christ."
I couldn't have expressed
it
any better.

I tipped him a quarter
and drove off
east on Hollywood Boulevard
and then I
took a right at
Vermont.

combat primer

they called Céline a Nazi
they called Pound a fascist
they called Hamsun a Nazi and a fascist.
they put Dostoevsky in front of a firing
squad
and they shot Lorca
gave Hemingway electric shock treatments
(and you know he shot himself)
and they ran Villon out of town (Paris)
and Mayakovsky
disillusioned with the regime
and after a lovers' quarrel,
well,
he shot himself too.
Chatterton took rat poison
and it worked.
and some say Malcolm Lowry died
choking on his own vomit
while drunk.
Crane went the way of the boat
propellor or the sharks.

Harry Crosby's sun was black.
Berryman preferred the bridge.
Plath didn't light the oven.

Seneca cut his wrists in the
bathtub (it's best that way:
in warm water).
Thomas and Behan drank themselves
to death and
there are many others.

and you want to be a
writer?

it's that kind of war:
creation kills,
many go mad,
some lose their way and
can't do it
anymore.
a few make it to old age.
a few make money.
some starve (like Vallejo).
it's that kind of war:
casualties everywhere.

all right, go ahead
do it
but when they sandbag you
from the blind side
don't come to me with your
regrets.

now I'm going to smoke a cigarette
in the bathtub
and then I'm going to
sleep.

thanks for that

at this time
I no longer have to work
the nightclubs and the universities
the bookstores
for tiny checks.
I no longer have to tell the freshman English class
at the U. of Nebraska (Omaha)
while sitting with my hangover at 11 a.m.
at a brown elevated desk
why I did it
how I did it
and what they might do in order to do
it too.

but I didn't mind the plane flights back home
with the businessmen
all of us drinking doubles
and trying not to look out past the wing
trying to relax
each happy that we were not on skid row
knowing we each had a certain talent
(so far)
which had saved us from that
(so far).

I may have to do it again some day but
right now I am where I belong:
flying over my own Mississippi River
passing over my own Grand Canyon
on schedule
no seat belt
no stewardess and
no lost luggage.

they arrived in time

I like to think about writers like James Joyce
Hemingway, Ambrose Bierce, Faulkner, Sherwood
Anderson, Jeffers, D. H. Lawrence, A. Huxley,
John Fante, Gorki, Turgenev, Dostoevsky, Saroyan,
Villon, even Sinclair Lewis, and Hamsun, even T. S.
Eliot and Auden, William Carlos Williams and
Stephen Spender and gutsy Ezra Pound.

they taught me so many things that my parents
never taught me, and
I also like to think of Carson McCullers
with her *Sad Cafe* and *Golden Eye.*
she too taught me much that my parents
never knew.

I liked to read the hardcover library books
in their simple library bindings
blue and green and brown and light red
I liked the older librarians (male and female)
who stared seriously at one
if you coughed or laughed too loudly,
and even though they looked like my parents
there was no real resemblance.

now I no longer read those authors I once read
with such pleasure,
but it's good to think about them,
and I also
like to look again at photographs of Hart Crane and
Caresse Crosby at Chantilly, 1929
or at photographs of D. H. Lawrence and Frieda
sunning at Le Moulin, 1928.

I like to see André Malraux in his flying outfit
with a kitten on his chest and
I like photos of Artaud in the madhouse
Picasso at the beach with his strong legs
and his hairless head, and then there's
D.H. Lawrence milking that cow
and Aldous at Saltwood Castle, Kent, August
1963.

I like to think about these people
they taught me so many things that I
never dreamed of before.
and they taught me well,
very well
when it was so much needed
they showed me so many things
that I never knew were possible.
those friends
deep in my blood
who
when there was no chance
gave me one.

odd

some nights
like this night
seem to crawl down the back of one's
neck and settle at the base of the skull,
stay there
like that
like this.
it is probably a little prelude to
death,
a warm-up.
I accept.
then the mind becomes like a
movie:
I watch Dostoevsky in a small room
and he is drinking a glass of
milk.
it is not a long movie:
he puts the glass down and it
ends.
then I am back
here.
an air purifier
makes its soft sound behind me.
I smoke too much, the whole room
often turns blue
so now my wife has put in the
air purifier.

now the night has left the back
of my skull.
I lean back in the swivel
chair

pick up a bottle opener shaped
like a horse.
it's like I'm holding the whole world
here
shaped like a horse.

I put the world down,
open a paper clip and begin to clean
my fingernails.

waiting on death can be perfectly
peaceful.

an interlude

it was on Western Avenue
last night
about 7:30 p.m.
I was walking south
toward Sunset
and on the 2nd floor of
a motel across the street
in the apartment in front
the lights were on
and there was this young man
he must have weighed 400 pounds
he looked 7 feet tall
and 4 feet wide
as he reached over
and rather lazily punched
a naked woman in the face.
another woman jumped up
(this woman was fully clothed)
and he gave her a whack across
the back of the head before he
turned and punched the naked one
in the face again.
there was no screaming and
he seemed almost bored by it all.
then he walked over to the window
and opened it.
he had what looked like
a small roasted chicken in his
hand.
he put it to his mouth
bit nearly half of it away
and began chewing.

he chewed for a moment or
two
then spit the bones carefully
out the window
(I could hear them
fall on the
sidewalk).

good god jesus christ almighty,
have mercy on us all!

then he looked down at me
and smiled
as I quickly moved away
ducking my head down
into the night.

anonymity

I never got to where I was
driving that night after
I exhaled two 15's on the breath
meter.
they put the cuffs
on me
and I climbed into the back seat
of their squad car
for a ride to the drunk tank at
150 N. Los Angeles Street,
Parker Center.

"what's your occupation?"
the one not driving asked
me.

"I'm a writer," I answered.

"you sure don't look like a
writer to me," said the
cop.

"oh, I'm famous," I
said.

"I never heard of you,"
he said.

"I never heard of you either,"
I replied.

they parked, got me out and

walked me up the ramp.

"you sure don't look like a
writer," the cop said
again.

inside they took the cuffs
off.
I guess they were right:
I wasn't famous
and they weren't sure
what a writer should
look like.
but I knew what cops
looked like.
these were cops
and they were famous
and looked the same
all over the
world.

in a crowded drunk tank
everything was as per usual:
one toilet without a lid
and one pay
telephone, both
being used.

what's it all mean?

o yes Huxley motorcaded through southern Europe
and wrote a marvelous book about it and Lawrence
made that great painting of a man pissing
and Huxley did the peyote thing and Frieda really
gave Lawrence a *base* and Huxley said, "it's up here!"
touching his head and Lawrence said, "it's down here!"
touching his gut.
Huxley went blind you know and Lawrence had a
sixth sense when it came
to animals and
sometimes I think of Lawrence sometimes I think of
Huxley and sometimes I think of Charo with all that
hair on her head so chi-chi sexy and
then sometimes I think of 2 Mexican boys punching it
out down at the Olympic auditorium o yes
we've got a world full of dreams and sometimes
when I can't sleep
and my mind won't think of anything at all then I
spend the night
looking up at the dark ceiling.

one-to-five

I know horse racing.

I was there when Porterhouse beat Swaps and
that's a while back and
I've seen some more since.

so there I was in the stands
when the 8th race opened with a one-to-2 favorite on
the program.

"a lock," the boys liked to call it
but the boys all had rundown heels on their
shoes.

the favorite was a horse they fondly called
Big Cat. actually its name was Cougar II.
he had beaten the same horses while carrying high
        weight
had beaten them easily
and now in this race
each horse was to carry 126 pounds.

Cougar read one-to-2 on the program and one-to-5 on
        the board.

they applauded him as he walked in the post parade.

I put a deuce on the 2nd favorite who read
8-to-one and waited on the
race.

it was a mile-and-one-half on the grass.

the gate opened and they came down the hill with
Big Cat laying up near the pace—3rd or 4th—
he looked in good position until after they
went down the backstretch and got near the final curve.

Big Cat began falling back.

what the hell was Pincay doing?

cries went up from the stands:
"he isn't going to make it!"
"my god, he isn't going to make it!"

then Big Cat seemed to come on again
he had the only red silks in the race
he was very visible out there.

maybe Pincay knew what he was doing:
he was the #1 jock on the #1
horse

but by then
Big Spruce
(at 13-to-one off a morning line of 6)
had run past the early pace setters and
was opening up
12 lengths
halfway down the stretch.

no chance for Big Cat.

Big Spruce won
easily

while Big Cat
had to wait out the photo for
3rd money.

I checked the total on Big Cat off the tote:
over one-half million dollars.

Pincay got sick and scratched out of the
9th race.

Eddie Arcaro
who carried one of the meanest whips in racing
and had ridden them all
once said:
"there's no such thing as a sure thing."

(as the history of the world will tell you—
the easier it looks
the harder it gets).

Big Cat lost.

nobody applauded his walk back to the
barn.

in this world
you just can't lose at
one-to-5

anyhow
not with grace

no matter how many
you've won before
that

especially not in
America

nor in Paris or
Spain

nor in Munich or
Japan

nor anywhere else where
humans
dwell.

insanity

sometimes there's a crazy one in the street.
he lifts his feet carefully as he walks.
he ponders the mystery
of his own anus.
while the American dollar collapses
against the German mark
he's thinking of Bette Davis and her old movies.

it's good to bring thought to bear on things
arcane and forbidden.
if only we were crazy enough
to be willing to ignore our
mechanical and static perceptions
we'd know that a half-filled coffee cup
holds more secrets
than, say,
the Grand Canyon.

sometimes there's a crazy one walking
in the street.
he slips past
walks with a black crow on his shoulder
is not worried about alarm clocks or
approval.

however, almost everybody else is sane, knows the
answers to all the unanswerable questions.
we can park our automobiles
carve a turkey with style and
can laugh at every feeble joke.

the crazy ones only laugh when there is

no reason to
laugh.

in our world
the sane are too numerous,
too submissive.
we are instructed to live lives of boredom.
no matter what we are doing—
screwing or eating or playing or
talking or climbing mountains or
taking baths or flying to India
we are numbed,
sadly sane.

when you see a crazy one walking
in the street
honor him but
leave him alone.
stand out of the way.
there's no luck like that luck
nothing else so perfect in the world
let him walk untouched
remember that Christ also was insane.

farewell my lovely

she keeps coming back
with different men
I am introduced
and I feel sorry for them
sitting there in their pants and
shirts and stockings and shoes
looking out of their heads with
their eyes
hearing with their ears
speaking out of their mouths
I feel sorry for them
for she is finally going to do to
them
just what she did to me.
she hates men but captures and tortures them
with her beautiful, youthful body.

the last time she was over
she followed me
into the kitchen
leaving him sitting alone out there.
"I miss you," she said, "I really
do. I mean it."

I knew what she missed. she missed
having a man securely caught in her
net. I stepped around her with
the drinks and walked back into the
other room.

she watched me with her eyes
as she continued to talk.
she had watched me go crazy with the

agony of losing her
so many times before.
now she knew I was free
and when the victim escapes the
executioner
it is hell for the
executioner.

she felt it. she said to him,
"let's get out of here."

they left and began to walk away
toward the street.
I noticed she had left her coat, the
one with the dark
hood.

"hey!" I shouted, "you left your
coat!"
she ran back to the door:
"oh, *thank* you!" she said
taking the coat with one
hand
and with the other hand
behind the door
where he couldn't see
she gave me the
finger,
vigorously.

I closed the door.
it hadn't been too
bad
they hadn't used up much of
my time
at most
maybe fifteen
minutes.

comments upon my last book of poesy:

you're better than ever.
you've sold out.
you suck.
my mother hates you.
you're rich.
you're the best writer in the English language.
can I come see you?
I write just like you do, only better.
why do you drive a BMW?
why don't you give more readings?
can you still get it up?
do you know Allen Ginsberg?
what do you think of Henry Miller?
will you write a foreword to my next book?
I enclose a photograph of Céline.
I enclose my grandfather's pocket watch.
the enclosed jacket was knitted by my wife in Bavarian
      style.
have you been drunk with Mickey Rourke?
I am a young girl 19 years old and I will come and clean
      your house.
you are a stinking bastard to tell people that Shakespeare is
      not readable.
what do you think of Norman Mailer?
why do you steal from Hemingway?
why do you knock Tolstoy?
I'm doing hard time and when I get out I'm coming to see
      you.
I think you suck ass.
you've saved my god-damned life.
why do you hate women?
I love you.

I read your poems at parties.
did all those things really happen to you?
why do you drink?
I saw you at the racetrack but I didn't bother you.
I'd like to renew our relationship.
do you really stay up all night?
I can out-drink you.
you stole it from Sherwood Anderson.
did you ever meet Ezra?
I am alone and I think of you every night.
who the hell do you think you're fooling?
my tits aren't much but I've got great legs.
fuck you, man.
my wife hates you.
will you please read the enclosed poems and comment?
I am going to publish all those letters you wrote me.
you jack-off motherfuck, you're not fooling anybody.

a correction to a lady of poesy:

"I think all life is a matter of luck—good and bad."—Diane Wakoski

any ballplayer can tell you, Diane:
in games like baseball where luck is just a percentage,
        even
there it evens
out—
dribble one through the shortpatch for a single and your
        next one
might be a line drive into the 2nd baseman's mitt.

in games unlike baseball
in games like life
one good man might survive while another dies
but this isn't luck
this is making a connection
hitting the ball solidly on the nose.
(but even the good man making the connection seldom
        remains the good
man—he often softens in time and finally
fails).

if you consider yourself lucky,
don't,
for whatever you've gained you've gained by
doing something a little differently or
with a little more magic than
somebody else.
but when the magic goes·or
lessens, and it usually
does, and

when the poetry readings drop off
and the publishers stop inquiring as to your next
manuscript, will you then consider your luck
bad?
will you then start bitching about
the unfairness of the game
like some untalented scribblers (not you)
who I know?

see the old ladies in the supermarkets
angry and lonely
pushing their carts—
that they were once given young bodies was not luck
or that they lost them was not,
or that they did not build a life on something firmer
was not.

I am for the survival of all people until
natural age takes
them. but they'll need something more than luck, and a
     cunning better than
poetry.
it's hardly luck when the spider takes a fly or bad luck
     when the fly
enters the web.

I could go on
but I feel by now
I've made the point,
and as the people come home this evening
from the war
and sit at their tables to eat and
talk, and perhaps later to make
love
(if they are not too tired)
don't tell them that all life is a matter of luck—
good and bad.

they know it's a matter of
doing or dying.
Hitler, Ty Cobb, the man at the vegetable stand—
they knew it and they know it.

save the bad luck fairy tale for small
children. they'll learn the real story
soon enough.

Beethoven conducted his last symphony
while totally deaf

his paintings would not be as valuable
now
if he hadn't
sliced off his ear
worn that rag around his head
and then done it to himself
among the cornstalks.

and would that one's poems be
so famous if he hadn't
faded at 19,
given it all up to
go gun running and gold hunting
in Africa only to
die of syphilis?

what about the one who was
murdered in the road
by Spanish fascists?
did that
give his words more
meaning?

or take the one who was a
national hero
those iceberg symphonies soaring
cutting that particular sky
in half
he had it all working for him
then he got worried about old age
saved his head

went into his house
vanished and was never seen
again.

such strange behavior, didn't somebody
once say?

that the man should be as durable as his
art, that's what they want, they want the
impossible: creation and creator to be as
one. this is the dirty trick
of the ages.

on the sidewalk and in the sun

I have seen an old man around town recently
carrying an enormous pack.
he uses a walking stick
and moves up and down the streets
with this pack strapped to his back.

I keep seeing him.

if he'd only throw that pack away, I think,
he'd have a chance, not much of a chance
but a chance.

and he's in a tough district—east Hollywood.
they aren't going to give him a
dry bone in east Hollywood.

he is lost. with that pack.
on the sidewalk and in the sun.

god almighty, old man, I think, throw away that
pack.

then I drive on, thinking of my own
problems.

the last time I saw him he was not walking.
it was ten thirty a.m. on north Bronson and
hot, very hot, and he sat on a little ledge, bent,
the pack still strapped to his back.

I slowed down to look at his face.
I had seen one or two other men in my life

with looks on their faces like
that.

I speeded up and turned on the
radio.

I knew that look.

I would never see him again.

what do they want?

there are times when those eyes inside your
brain stare back at
you;
it is always sudden.
sometimes when you come in
and lie down on the bed
it happens—
2 eyes that have nothing to do with
you
stare back at you from inside your
brain.
you sit up
until they go away.

or say you scream at a child
or slap a woman—
as you walk into the kitchen
the eyes appear in the back of your brain
hang there
as you drink
water.

or sometimes you are at peace
sitting on a park bench
reading a newspaper—
here come the
eyes:
fat red golden eyes,
a pair.
you get up and
walk
away.

or the phone rings and as you answer the
phone
the eyes arrive again—
"yes, of course. no, I'm not doing
anything. yeh, I feel
o.k."
then you hang up, go to the bathroom and
throw water on
your face.

I would gladly give these eyes to the
blind or to anybody who
would take them.

o, o, there they are
again.

I don't understand it.
what do they
want?

I hear all the latest hit tunes

somewhere in whatever neighborhood
there's
some guy
at 10:30 in the morning
sunday morning
monday morning
any morning

washing and polishing his
car
with the radio on
LOUD
so that the entire neighborhood
is compelled
to listen to the music
that he is
listening to
but it's all right
because we surely don't
want him to be bored out
there;
it's going to take him
hours.

they'd arrest a drunk or a
panhandler
as a
public nuisance
but this boy is a
respectable citizen
and it's the respectable
citizens

that our culture is built
upon
and whom
the music is written
for.

if I murdered him
no court in America would
forgive
my courage.

meanwhile
he circles his car
with the
hose plus
a bucket of
suds.

he's safe
he's fearless
look at him there
almost as handsome as that twittering
bluejay
and at least 4 women are
in love with
him and he
deserves them all
and I hope he
gets them all.

it's the only way we can
teach that
son-of-a-bitch what
suffering is.

am I the only one who suffers thus?

took me 45 minutes to find my glasses,
and I lost a credit card mailed to me today,
then I sat down at this machine and it wouldn't
function,
took me 15 minutes to put it back in
order.

yes, I am constantly losing things and
the fault is mine,
I sit in this room and it is a collection of
trash—
papers, wine bottle corks, scotch tape,
magazines, letters, bills, old wrist
watches and sundry other items
which rest one upon the
other:
paint tubes, toothpicks,
non-functioning cigarette lighters,
liquid paper, pens, address labels,
boxes of light bulbs, a red toy devil,
a wall socket (for 3 prongs), matchbooks,
lens cleaning tissue, 25 cent stamps (they
are now 29 cents and rising),
bottle openers, band-aids, well, I just don't
know what else.

I suppose the saddest of all are the letters
from lonely people
(and look, here are two pocket combs
resting side by side)
and then there's the telephone and
the answering machine taking the

messages:
more lonely people, more frustrated
people, more eager people,
more people wanting to come by,
wanting to talk ...
how can they find TIME to talk?
I don't have time to do the simplest
things.
in my wallet there is a piece of paper:
IN CASE OF ACCIDENT OR DEATH,
PLEASE INFORM, ETC.
for 3 years now I have been wanting
to take this piece of paper out of my
wallet and update it,
because all the phone numbers and
addresses except one
have changed
yet I haven't been able to attend to
this matter.
also, I know that the spare tire
in my car needs a bit of
air.
but when?
when will I do it?
when will I get my teeth cleaned?
when will I cut my toenails?
when will I get a haircut?
there are countless other untended
matters
while the IRS and the California Franchise Tax Board
loom ...

and still there are people who come by here
and plant themselves upon the couch
and they seem to have absolutely
NOTHING to do
but

chat away.
chat, chat, chat about absolutely
nothing.
or they want to play GAMES or watch the
damnedest garbage on TV
(I've been waiting to shine my shoes
for a year now)
or they work crossword puzzles
or tell jokes.

every time there is a knock at the
door
a deathly chill runs up my
back:
it will be one of them,
it is always one of them
and when they come in and ease
down on that couch
I am truly in hell.

I do all that I can to keep
them away
but through one guise or
another
or through some affiliation,
they slip
through.
and they are aware of it,
they are very aware of
it
and then they begin...

my life, at that moment,
becomes only a process of
waiting for them to
leave
and their life becomes

a process of staying
as long as
possible.

and one must not hurt
their feelings
for they would not
understand!

on lighting a cigar

we ask for no mercy and no
miracles;
(if only there were fewer flies around
as we ponder our imbecilities and losses!)

I light a cigar, lean back
remember
dead friends dead days dead loves;
so much has gone by for most of us,
even the young, especially the young
for they have lost the beginning and have
the rest of the way to go;
but isn't it strange, all I can think of now are
cucumbers, oranges, junk yards, the
old Lincoln Heights jail and
the lost loves that went so hard
and almost brought us to the edge,
the faces now without features,
the love beds forgotten.

the mind is kind: it retains the
important things:
cucumbers
oranges
junk yards
jails.

I have killed a fly
that tiny piece of life
dead like dead love.

there used to be over 100 of us in that big room

in that jail
I was in there many
times.
you slept on the floor
men stepped on your face on the way to piss.
always a shortage of cigarettes.
names called out during the night
(the few lucky ones who were bailed out)
never you.

we asked for no mercy or miracles
and we ask for none
now;
we paid our way, laugh if you will,
we walked the only paths there were to walk.

and when love came to us twice
and lied to us twice
we decided to never love again
that was fair
fair to us
and fair to love itself.

we ask for no mercy or no
miracles;
we are strong enough to live
and to die and to
kill flies,

attend the boxing matches, go to the racetrack,
live on luck and skill,
get alone, get alone often,
and if you can't sleep alone
be careful of the words you speak in your sleep;
        and
ask for no mercy
no miracles;

and don't forget:
time is meant to be wasted,
love fails
and death is useless.

the cigarette of the sun

the headless dog snaps,
the half melon drips, there's blood under the
fingernails,
the yawweed cries and
Tacitus hops like a frog.
destitution everywhere,
the manacled in rusted armor walk through
crippled dreams,
one more dead. one more dying. one more to die.
they lied to themselves and then to us and then to the
    stinking wind.
bargain basement heroes erected for elucidation.
poison music stuffs the brain,
the roses yell for mercy,
mouse chases cat,
elephants carry the gray bad news,
infinity is split and nothing happens
and
one more dead. one more dying. one more to die.
the engine is stuffed with peat moss.
the schoolboys eat gravel.
space mutilates space.
the pin worms dance with the collared peccary.
throats are cut like bread.
flags are covered with custard.
the knife chases the gun.
and
one more
dead.
dying.
to die.
one more dead

rose
dog
flea
hyena,
as the spoon and the feather
dance in the night,
as the sheet pulls up the hand,
as the twilight laughs for its pill.
one more sister cut in half.
one more brother stuffed in the
bin.
the shoes put on you.
you, you, you,
no más, no more.

to lean back into it

like in a chair the color of the sun
as you listen to lazy piano music
and the aircraft overhead are not
at war.
where the last drink is as good as
the first
and you realized that the promises
you made yourself were
kept.
that's plenty.
that last: about the promises:
what's not so good is that the few
friends you had are
dead and they seem
irreplaceable.
as for women, you didn't know enough
early enough
and you knew enough
too late.
and if more self-analysis is allowed: it's
nice that you turned out well-
honed,
that you arrived late
and remained generally
capable.
outside of that, not much to say
except you can leave without
regret.
until then, a bit more amusement,
a bit more endurance,
leaning back
into it.

like the dog who got across
the busy street:
not all of it was good
luck.

dog fight 1990

he draws up to my rear bumper in the fast lane.
I can see his face in the rear view mirror, his eyes
are blue and he sucks on a dead cigar.
I pull over. he passes, then slows. I don't like
this.
I pull into the fast lane, ride
his rear bumper. we are as a team passing through
Compton.
I turn the radio on and light a cigarette.
he ups it 5 mph, I do likewise. we are as a team
entering Inglewood.
he pulls out of the fast lane and I drive past.
then I slow. when I check the rear view mirror he is
on my bumper again.
he has almost made me miss my turnoff at Century Blvd.
I hit the blinker and fire across 3 lanes of
traffic, just make the off-ramp,
cutting in front of an inflammable tanker.
blue eyes comes from behind the tanker and
we veer down the ramp in separate lanes to the signal.
we sit there side by side, not looking at each
other.
I am caught behind an empty school bus as he idles
behind a Mercedes.
the signal switches and he is gone. I cut to the
inside lane behind him. then I see the parking
lane open and I flash by to the right of him and the
Mercedes, turn up the radio, make the green light as the
Mercedes and blue eyes run the yellow turning into red.
they make it as I switch back ahead of
them in order to miss a parked vegetable
truck.

now we are running 1-2-3, not a cop in sight. we are
moving through a 1990 California July.
we are driving with skillful nonchalance.
we are moving in perfect formation.
we are as a team
approaching L.A. airport.
1-2-3
2-3-1
3-2-1.

I used to feel sorry for Henry Miller

when he got old he stopped writing, dabbled with
paints and put ads in the UCLA paper for
secretarial help.
Henry preferred Oriental ladies, young
ones
and they came by and did little things for
him
and he fell in love with them,
even though there was no sex.
he wrote them letters, all his writing went into
love letters.
and the ladies were flattered but simply went
on
teasing him.
he liked having them around.
maybe he felt that they held death back a
little
or maybe they stopped him from thinking
about it too much
or maybe the old boy was simply
horny.

I remember a young lady who came to
see me who said,
"I was going to fuck Henry Miller before he
died but now it's too late so I came to see
you."
"forget it, baby," I told her.

I liked the way Henry Miller looked in his
last years, like a wise Buddha
but he didn't act like one.

I only wish he had gone out in a
different way,
not begging for it,
using his name.

I would have preferred to see him
continue to write books
until the end,
right into the face
of death.

but since he couldn't do it
well, maybe somebody else
can.
there's some old fart
somewhere,
I'm sure
who can.

if he doesn't diddle his brains
away at the
racetrack.

locked in

morning,
it touches the nerves
quickly
as if we were already in
the hunter's sights.
the body yawns and stretches in the
light.
the pilgrimage
is about to
begin.

padding to the bathroom
to eliminate the
poisons.
behind the curtains is
their world.

wash hands, neck, face,
brush the remaining teeth
for the remaining
days.

clothe thyself.
not *that* shirt!
it's depressing...
get something green, something
yellow.
there, look.
smile.

shoes, damned shoes.
shoes look so sad.

you can't hide facts from
shoes.
forget the shoes,
put on your stupid shorts.
your fat buttery pants.

now, the shoes.

you forgot your hair.
comb your hair.
you look crazy with your hair
uncombed.
you're not crazy, are
you?

your wife is still asleep.
you're lucky.
she's lucky.
smile.
you're not crazy, are
you?

you go downstairs.
the animals wait for you.
the plants look at you
while the termites eat the wood.
the ant army beneath,
the poisoned air above.
your car outside.
your intestines, your belly,
your heart, your brain, your
etc.
inside.

you're sane,
you're normal.
you make sensible

decisions?

only there's a limit.
that's the catch.
you're the catch.
caught.

is it better to be a termite?
an ocelot?
a metronome?
a park bench?
or East Kansas City?

I feed the animals.
for that moment, that is what
I do.
I feed the animals.
it's
easy.

wasted

too often the people complain that they have
done nothing with their
lives
and then they wait for somebody to tell them
that this isn't so.
look, you've done this and that and you've
done that and that's
something.
you really think so?
of course.

but
they had it right.
they've done nothing.
shown no courage.
no inventiveness.
they did what they were taught to
do.
they did what they were told to
do.
they had no resistance, no thoughts
of their own.
they were pushed and shoved
and went obediently.
they had no heart.
they were cowardly.
they stank in life.
they stank up life.

and now they want to be told that
they didn't fail.
you've met them.

they're everywhere.
the spiritless.
the dead-before-death gang.

be kind?
lie to them?
tell them what they want to hear?
tell them anything they want to hear?

people with courage made them what they
aren't.

and if they ask me, I'll tell them what they
don't want to hear.

it's better you
keep them away from me, or
they'll tell you I'm a cruel man.

it's better that they confer
with you.

I want to be free of
that.

Sunday lunch at the Holy Mission

he got knifed in broad daylight, came up the street
holding his hands over his gut, dripping red
on the pavement.
nobody waiting in line left their place to help him.
he made it to the Mission doorway, collapsed in the
lobby where the desk clerk screamed, "hey, you
son-of-a-bitch, what are you doing?"
then he called an ambulance but the man was dead
when they got there.
the police came and circled the spots of blood
on the pavement
with white chalk
photographed everything
then asked the men waiting for their Sunday meal
if they had seen anything
if they knew anything.
they all said "no" to both.

while the police strutted in their uniforms
the others finally loaded the body into an ambulance.

afterwards the homeless men rolled cigarettes
as they waited for their meal
talking about the action
blowing farts and smoke
enjoying the sun
feeling quite like
celebrities.

slaughter

the first seven rows were roped off for the Counselors
of Exceptional Children, the Frequent Flyers Club, and the
German Society.
it was Saturday at the track and they were all talking
at once, standing up, sitting down, waving, laughing.

when the winner of the first race came in, most of them
leaped up and down screaming and some of them hugged
one another.
it was difficult to believe that they had all bet on the same
horse.

I tried to separate the Counselors of Exceptional Children
    from the
Frequent Flyers and the Germans
but they all looked very much alike and as each race
went by they became quieter and quieter, and some of them
began to leave.

by the last race only a few of them remained
and they looked tired and very sad and were quiet.
they had learned a hard truth: losing one's money was very
much like death
and although the horses were beautiful, it was much easier
being German or an Exceptional Children's Counselor
or to fly around the country at reduced rates.

they had also learned that sometimes
the racetrack was no place to jump up and down
in, no place to scream in and to hug one another.
it got dark and cold as the wind came down off
the Sierra Madre, and as they put the horses into the gate

for the last race, even a winner wouldn't help much
now as the tote machines were shut down, taking the last
        bite,
freezing the odds forever.

favorites don't win enough
longshots don't win enough
the rest of the horses don't win enough.

next Saturday they'll bring in 3 new groups
and rope them off too.

a vote for the gentle light

burned senseless by other people's constant
depression,
I pull the curtains apart,
aching for the gentle light.
it's there, it's there
somewhere,
I'm sure.

oh, the faces of depression, expressions
pulled down into the gluey dark.
the bitter small sour mouths,
the self-pity, the self-justification is
too much, all too much.
the faces in shadow,
deep creases of gloom.

there's no courage there, just the desire to
possess something—admiration, fame, lovers,
money, any damn thing
so long as it comes easy.
so long as they don't have to do
what's necessary.
and when they don't succeed they
become embittered,
ugly,
they imagine that they have
been slighted, cheated,
demeaned.

then they concentrate upon their
unhappiness, their last
refuge.

and they're good at that,
they are very good at that.
they have so much unhappiness
they insist upon your sharing it
too.

they bathe and splash in their
unhappiness,
they splash it upon you.

it's all they have.
it's all they want.
it's all they can be.

you must refuse to join them.
you must remain yourself.
you must open the curtains
or the blinds
or the windows
to the gentle light.
to joy.
it's there in life
and even in death
it can be
there.

be alone

when you think about how often
it all goes wrong
again and again
you begin to look at the walls
and yearn to stay inside
because the streets are the
same old movie
and the heroes all end up like
old movie heroes:
fat ass, fat face and the brain
of a lizard.

it's no wonder that
a wise man will
climb a 10,000 foot mountain
and sit there waiting
living off of berry bush leaves
rather than bet it all on two dimpled knees
that surely won't last a lifetime
and 2 times out of 3
won't remain even for one long night.

mountains are hard to climb.
thus the walls are your friends.
learn your walls.

what they have given us out there
in the streets
is something that even children
get tired of.

stay within your walls.

they are the truest love.

build where few others build.
it's the last way left.

I inherit

the old guy next door died
last week,
he was 95 or 96,
I am not sure.
but I am now the oldest fart
in the neighborhood.
when I bend over to
pick up the morning
paper
I think of heart attack
or when I swim in my
pool
alone
I think,
Jesus Christ,
they'll come and
find me floating here
face down,
my 8 cats sitting on the
edge
licking and
scratching.
dying's not bad,
it's that little transition
from here to
there
that's strange
like flicking the light
switch
off.

I'm now the old fart

in the neighborhood,
been working at it for
some time,
but now I have to work
in some new
moves:
I have to forget to zip up
all the way,
wear slippers instead of my
shoes,
hang my glasses around my
neck,
fart loudly in the
supermarket,
wear unmatched
socks,
back my car into a
garbage can.
I must shorten my
stride, take small
mincing steps,
develop a squint,
bow my head and
ask, "what? what
did you say?"

I've got to get ready,
whiten my hair,
forget to
shave.
I want you to know me
when you see
me:
I'm now the old fart
in the neighborhood
and you can't tell me
a damn thing I don't already

know.

respect your elders,
sonny, and get the
hell out of my
way!

another day

having the low-down blues and going
into a restaurant to eat.
you sit at a table.
the waitress smiles at you.
she's dumpy. her ass is too big.
she radiates kindness and sympathy.
live with her 3 months and a man would
know some real agony.
o.k., you'll tip her 15%.
you order a turkey sandwich and a
beer.
the man at the table across from you
has watery blue eyes and
a head like an elephant.
at a table further down are 3 men
with very tiny heads
and long necks
like ostriches.
they talk loudly of land development.
why, you think, did I ever come
in here when I have the low-down
blues?
then the waitress comes back with the sandwich
and she asks you if there will be anything
else?
and you tell her, no no no, this will be
fine.
then somebody behind you laughs.
it's a cork laugh filled with sand and
broken glass.

you begin eating the sandwich.

it's something.
it's a minor, difficult,
sensible action
like composing a popular song
to make a 14-year-old
weep.
you order another beer.
jesus, look at that guy
his hands hang down almost to his
knees and he's
whistling.
well, time to get out.
pick up the bill.
tip.
go to the register.
pay.
pick up a toothpick.
go out the door.
your car is still there.
and there are the 3 men with heads
and necks
like ostriches all getting into one
car.
they each have a toothpick and now
they are talking about
women.
they drive away first.
they drive away fast.
they're best, I guess.
it's an unbearably hot day.
there's a first-stage smog alert.
all the birds and plants are dead
or dying.

you start the engine.

tabby cat

he has on bluejeans and tennis shoes
and walks with two young girls
about his age.
every now and then he leaps
into the air and
clicks his heels together.

he's like a young colt
but somehow he also reminds me
more of a tabby cat.

his ass is soft and
he has no more on his mind
than a gnat.

he jumps along behind his girls
clicking his heels together.

then he pulls the hair of one
runs over to the other and
squeezes her neck.

he has fucked both of them and
is pleased with himself.
it has all happened
so easily for him.

and I think, ah,
my little tabby cat
what nights and days
wait for you.

your soft ass
will be your doom.
your agony
will be endless
and the girls
who are yours now
will soon belong to other men
who didn't get their cookies
and cream so easily and
so early.

the girls are practicing on you
the girls are practicing for other men
for someone out of the jungle
for someone out of the lion cage.

I smile as
I watch you walking along
clicking your heels together.

my god, boy, I fear for you
on that night
when you first find out.

it's a sunny day now.

jump
while you
can.

the gamblers

the young boys at the track, what are they
doing here?
6 or 7 of them running around, tearing up
their tickets, saying,
"shit! god damn! fuck it!"
they whirl about, they look like virgins,
they are going to bet again.
it's the same after each race:
"shit! god damn! fuck it!"

they leave after the last race,
skipping down the stairways like fairies,
they wear sneakers, little t-shirts, tight
pants.
put all 6 or 7 of them together and you
won't get 800 pounds.
they've never been to jail, they live
with their parents; they've never had to
work 8 to 5.

what are they doing here at the race track?
I mean, it's bad enough that my horse
fell in the 4th, snapped his left foreleg
and had to be shot.

I mean, any damn fool can go to the
race track and most damn fools do,
but these little boys hollering
"shit! god damn! fuck it!"

well, there's no war right now
we can't stick them into a uniform just yet
but wait a while.

the crowd

they love to huddle and chat away the
night as I pour them wine.
my wife doesn't seem to mind and my mother-
in-law fits in nicely.
little exchanges as the hours have
their arms and legs chopped off,
their heads tossed away.
I can't believe they are
sitting there.
I can't believe their words or their
laughter.
I have no idea why they are here.
I have invited nobody.
I am the husband.
I am to act civilized.
I am to behave like them.
but I will live past them.
this night will not turn me into them.

there was a time when I used to run such
out the door.
but then I would hear over and over
what a beast I had been.

so now I sit with them,
attempt to listen.
I even lend a word now and then.
they have no idea how I feel.

I am like a surgeon cutting into the rot,
examining a malignancy.
strangely, there is nothing to be learned.

"good night, good night, drive
carefully."

after they leave
the place reshapes itself,
the cats come out of hiding,
I have my first peaceful
moment.

my wife and I sit together.
I say nothing of the
departed.
the moon shines through
the glass doors
and the life left in me
gently surfaces.
I have survived them
one
more
time.

trouble in the night

she awakens me almost every night,
"Hank! HANK!"
shaking me ...
"yeh?" I ask.
"don't you hear that?"
"go to sleep ..."
"THERE'S SOMETHING ON THE STAIRS!"
"all right ..."
I get up, my feet are numb, my legs buckle
at the knees.

I have a switchblade, and also a stun
gun that can freeze a man for
15 minutes.
I bother with neither
just walk to the stairway
naked
not caring if I find a 9 foot
monster,
almost hoping to find one.

—halfway down the stairway
it's only the cat
clawing an old newspaper to
pieces.
he only wants to get out
into the night
and I let him
out.

I go back up.

sometimes I think my woman lives with me only
because she is afraid to live
alone.

"it was the cat," I say, climbing in.

"ARE YOU SURE?"

sometimes I have to conduct
a real room-to-room search
with all the lights on.
I stand naked outside of closet doors
and say,
"o.k., come on out, big bad thing!"

but this night I refuse.
"go to sleep," I say, "and
in the morning
we'll check everything out."

I can feel her rigid
beside me
listening to the sounds of the
night but I am soon
asleep.

I dream that I can fly.
I flap my arms and I can fly gracefully
through the air.
below me men and women are running.
they curse me and throw objects.
they want me to come down.
they want my box of matches,
my camera and my
car keys.

but what does she want?

3 old men at separate tables

I am
one of them.
how did we get here?
where are our ladies?
what happened to
our lives and years?

this appears to be a calm Sunday
evening.
the waiters move among us.
we are poured water, coffee, wine.
bread arrives, armless, eyeless bread.
peaceful bread.
we order.
we await our orders.

where have the wars gone?
where have, even, the tiny agonies
gone?
this place has found us.
the white table cloths are placid ponds,
the utensils glimmer for our
fingers.

such calm is ungodly but
fair.
for in a moment we still remember the
hard years and those to come.
nothing is forgotten, it is merely put
aside.
like a glove, a gun, a
nightmare.

3 old men at separate tables.

eternity could be like this.

I lift my cup of coffee,
the centuries enduring
me,
nothing else matters so
sweetly
now.

the singer

this then
is the arena
forevermore.
this then is the arena
where you must
succeed or fail.

you have had some
success here
but they expect more
than that
in this arena.

there have been defeats too,
befuddling defeats.
there is no mercy in this
arena,
there is only victory or
defeat,
something living or something
dead.

this arena
is neither just
nor good.
there is no permanent
escape from this
arena.

and each temporary escape
has a permanent price.

neither drink nor love
will
see you through.

in this arena
now
stretching your arms
looking out the window
watching cats and leaves and shadows
thinking of vanished women and old automobiles
while Europe runs up and down your rug

you can only sing popular melodies
in the last of your mind.

stuck with it

this is plagiarism, of course, sitting here with
my hands and my feet,
sitting here lighting another deadly
cigarette,
then pouring more deathly booze into
myself,
and this is plagiarism
because I used to read Pound to my
drunken prostitute, my first
love.
I just didn't know, still don't.
I buried her, went on to
others,
then got married in Las Vegas,
and lost.

what we'd all like to do, of
course, is to cut through the
fog of centuries
and get down into where it
shines and blazes,
blazes and shines,
roars.
I gave it a shot,
missed.

I go to CoCo's,
get my Senior Citizen's
Dinner,
good deal, soup or salad,
the beverage, the main
course, cornbread

too.
and I sit with the
other old
farts,
listen to them
talk,
not bad, really, they've also
been burned down to the
nub.

now I sit here
plagiarizing, still probably
zapped by the Key West
Cuba Kid Fisherman
who opted out over his
last orange juice
somewhere in
Idaho.

we all steal.
but I'll tell you
the plagiarism I like best
is this pouring of the
cabernet sauvignon,
1988
from the
Alexander Valley.
and once I held a woman's
hand as she was dying of
cancer in a small room on
some 2nd floor
and the stink of it spread
for a thousand yards
everywhere
and I tried not to breathe.
my mother, your mother,
anybody's mother

and she said, dying,
"Henry, why do you write
those terrible
words?"

action on the corner

a man hit a pregnant woman
he seemed to know her
knocked her down on the sidewalk
outside the Mexican food place
she was wearing a black dress with
orange dots
she fell on her back and screamed
she had a bloody nose
and the man was fat
powerful
in workingman's clothes
and a crowd gathered:
"what did you
hit her for?"
"it's not right! you shouldn't do
that!"
he just stood there
looking down at her
as she sobbed
the blood from her nose
running into her
mouth.
more people gathered
there must have been
15 people.
"somebody do something!" a woman
said.
nobody did.
just then an old battered black car
with the headlights on
at noon
came down the street at
70 m.p.h.

a bearded man was driving
swerving to avoid a car
he flashed by with 2 wheels
momentarily up on the
curb near the
crowd.
there were shouts:
"LOOK OUT!"
"JESUS!"
then he got the wheels back down
on the street
fired through the
red light
without hitting a thing and
was gone.
when the crowed recovered
and looked around again
the pregnant woman
was still on the
sidewalk
she looked almost
asleep
but the man was
gone.
"the son-of-a-bitch got
away," somebody
said.
one man looked up at the
sky
as if looking for an invasion
from space.
the cook from the Mexican cafe
stood in his
dirty apron.
then somebody moved forward and
helped the pregnant woman
to her feet.

no guru

I keep getting phone calls from the
helpless and the lonely and the
depressed.

yes, I tell them, that happens to all of
us.

oh, you're writing poems now? I'll buy your
book.

women? you lose them and you find
them. be strong. eat well.
sleep late, if
possible.

you're sick? you should jog, jog
along the water. watch for the
dolphins. you need vitamin E, cigarettes, and a
new typewriter ribbon.

I hang up.
I go over and sit down in front of the
typewriter.

little do they know, those suffering
bastards, that no man is completely
sane. I am sweating behind the ears.
the phone rings again. I
listen. I listen until it stops
then I lean over the
keys...

another great book in the works
for
Barnes and Noble.

in this cage some songs are born

I write poetry, worry, smile,
laugh
sleep
continue for a while
just like most of us
just like all of us;
sometimes I want to hug all
Mankind on earth
and say,
god damn all this that they've brought down
upon us,
we are brave and good
even though we are selfish
and kill each other and
kill ourselves,
we are the people
born to kill and die and weep in dark rooms
and love in dark rooms,
and wait, and
wait and wait and wait.
we are the people.
we are nothing
more.

my movie

my movies are getting better finally.
but I remember this one old movie I starred in.
I worked as a janitor in a tall office building
at night, with other men and
women who cleaned up the shit
left behind by other people.
those men and women had a very tired and dark and
useless feeling about them.

this one old man and I
we used to work very fast together
and then sit in an office on the top
floor
at the Big Man's desk
our feet up there as
we looked out over the city and
watched the sun come up while
drinking whiskey
from the Big Man's wet bar.
the old man talked and I listened to the
years of his life
not much
he was just another tired guy who cleaned up
other people's shit
and did a good job of it.

I didn't.
they canned me.

then I got a job as a dishwasher
and they also canned me there because
I wasn't a good dishwasher.

this was a seemingly endless low-budget movie
it ran for years and years
it didn't cost 50 million to make
it didn't have an anti-war message
it really didn't have much to say about anything
but you still ought to read my poems
and see it.

a new war

a different fight now, warding off the weariness of
age,
retreating to your room, stretching out upon the bed,
there's not much will to move,
it's near midnight now.

not so long ago your night would be just
beginning, but don't lament lost youth:
youth was no wonder
either.

but now it's the waiting on death.
it's not death that's the problem, it's the waiting.

you should have been dead decades ago.
the abuse you wreaked upon yourself was
enormous and non-ending.
a different fight now, yes, but nothing to
mourn, only to
note.

frankly, it's even a bit dull waiting on the
blade.

and to think, after I'm gone,
there will be more days for others, other days,
other nights.
dogs walking, trees shaking in
the wind.

I won't be leaving much.
something to read, maybe.

a wild onion in the gutted
road.

Paris in the dark.

roll the dice

if you're going to try, go all the
way.
otherwise, don't even start.

if you're going to try, go all the
way.
this could mean losing girlfriends,
wives, relatives, jobs and
maybe your mind.

go all the way.
it could mean not eating for 3 or
4 days.
it could mean freezing on a
park bench.
it could mean jail,
it could mean derision,
mockery,
isolation.
isolation is the gift,
all the others are a test of your
endurance, of
how much you really want to
do it.
and you'll do it
despite rejection and the
worst odds
and it will be better than
anything else
you can imagine.

if you're going to try,

go all the way.
there is no other feeling like
that.
you will be alone with the
gods
and the nights will flame with
fire.

do it, do it, do it.
do it.

all the way
all the way.

you will ride life straight to
perfect laughter, it's
the only good fight
there is.

PHOTO: Michael Montfort

CHARLES BUKOWSKI is one of America's best-known contemporary writers of poetry and prose, and, many would claim, its most influential and imitated poet. He was born in Andernach, Germany, to an American soldier father and a German mother in 1920, and brought to the United States at the age of three. He was raised in Los Angeles and lived there for fifty years. He published his first story in 1944 when he was twenty-four and began writing poetry at the age of thirty-five. He died in San Pedro, California, on March 9, 1994, at the age of seventy-three, shortly after completing his last novel, *Pulp* (1994).

During his lifetime he published more than forty-five books of poetry and prose, including the novels *Post Office* (1971), *Factotum* (1975), *Women* (1978), *Ham on Rye* (1982), and *Hollywood* (1989). Among his most recent books are the posthumous editions of *What Matters Most Is How Well You Walk Through the Fire* (1999), *Open All Night: New Poems* (2000), *Beerspit Night and Cursing: The Correspondence of Charles Bukowski and Sheri Martinelli 1960-1967* (2001), and *The Night Torn Mad with Footsteps: New Poems* (2001).

All of his books have now been published in translation in over a dozen languages and his worldwide popularity remains undiminished. In the years to come, Ecco will publish additional volumes of previously uncollected poetry and letters.

THESE AND OTHER TITLES BY CHARLES BUKOWSKI
ARE AVAILABLE FROM
ecco *An Imprint of HarperCollinsPublishers*

ISBN 0-06-057705-3 (hc)
ISBN 0-06-057706-1 (pb)

ISBN 0-06-057703-7 (hc)
ISBN 0-06-057704-5 (pb)

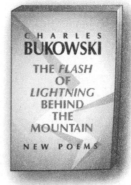

ISBN 0-06-057701-0 (hc)
ISBN 0-06-057702-9 (pb)

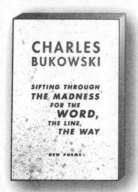

ISBN 0-06-052735-8 (hc)
ISBN 0-06-056823-2 (pb)

ISBN 0-876-85557-5 (pb)

ISBN 0-876-85362-9 (pb)

ISBN 0-876-85086-7 (pb)

ISBN 0-876-85926-0 (pb)

ISBN 0-876-85390-4 (pb)